I0537594

Community Service.

Timothy Conehead

The

Invincible.

Copyright © 2017 Kathleen Phythian.

All rights reserved.

978-0-9931076-8-9

ISBN-13:

Disclaimer.

This book is a work of pure fiction as are all Timothy's writings, it is full of lies lies and more lies and loaded with innuendo and even more lies. Some of the places in Community Service are real and some are imagined, some of the people are real and some are imagined. Events, businesses and incidents are either the product of the authors imagination or used in a fictitious manner. Any resemblance to actual persons living or dead or actual events is with permission or purely coincidental, this is a work of fiction. We really didn't see Lord Lucan or the Blue Meanies but we may have seen a headless horseman but we are not telling.

❤

DEDICATION

This book is dedicated to the memory of Laddie the Baddie who on 5th May 2017 aged 16 years 7 months took up residence at Rainbow Bridge, 9 months to the day that I said my last goodbye to Sir Lord Jack. Also to all the other border collies I have rescued loved and lost, there are now thirteen border collies all waiting up there for me to come and take them on a message. I hope they have big chariots there or I'll be in trouble. Not forgetting those I still have of course and at the time of writing I still have Princess Freya the Hunter, Timothy Conehead the Invincible and the newest edition to my family my first ever puppy Jennifer Eccles. [The Boss]

♥

The dedication continues to all rescues whether centre based or online including, Dogs Trust Merseyside for their ongoing support and for my first ever puppy, Jennifer. Also with special thanks to Dogs Trust Evesham Special needs unit, Freshfields Animal Rescue, Carla Lane Animals in Need, R.S,P,C.A. Liverpool, Protecting Preloved Border Collies, Lily's Border Collie Lifeline, Border Collie Rescue, Shamans Legacy Dog Rescue, Rescue Me Animal Sanctuary, Many Tears, The Freedom of Spirit Trust For Border Collies and The Border Collie Trust. All of the volunteers who help run these places and all the volunteer drivers who transport these lucky ones up, down and across the country.

You are all stars and I salute you.

♥

Without some of the above I would not have had the sheer pleasure and joy of loving and 'correcting' so many beautiful collies and being loved and herded back in return.

♥

Please support your local rescue centres or any of the many online rescues. No matter what breed you are after there will be a rescue centre with that breed in just waiting for your Love and to find their 'furever' home.

♥

If you can't adopt then please
Foster, if you can't foster then please
Sponsor, if you can't sponsor then please
Volunteer, if you can't volunteer then please
Donate, if can't donate then please
Educate, if you cannot do this then please
Share posts on social media and cross post if you can.

All of the above saves lives, you could save a life today simply by 'liking' a post and you could save more by sharing it.
Remember..

All you need is Love and Love is all you need.
Oh and a border collie or two or three or four..
Limitations exist Only in the Mind.

Love,
Kathleen
♥

INTRODUCTION.

I've been privileged to own, foster and rehabilitate many border collies throughout my life but never had one quite as young as Timothy. He was nine months old and an emergency rescue who I intended to foster for a short while until a forever home could be found for him. I was told that the poor lad had been kept initially locked in a bathroom and later muzzled and locked in a car. At that time I had two old codgers Sir Lord Jack who was my top dog and aged 16 and Laddie the Baddie who was 14, the day before Timothy arrived on my doorstep I had welcomed Freya into my home, she had been used for breeding I had been informed and then cast out when her last litter produced only one pup. There are some cruel callous people in this world.

To say he was a handful is an understatement. The boy was wild and had zero social skills whatsoever and all the energy of a border collie pup. Oh my, I did wonder if I had bitten off more than I could chew.

I love writing and so I decided to keep an online diary of his antics and many people enjoyed them so I carried on. I decided that he was in training to my oldest and most precious boy Sir Lord Jack of the Kingdom of Goodness and Love who could do no wrong. Laddie the Baddie would teach him how to be naughty and Princess Freya the Hunter would help me to keep him in check.

I am often told that Timothy's tales are hilarious, they are certainly full of innuendo as he misunderstands just about everything and then misinforms everyone of whats going on in his new home at 'Kathleen's School of Correction.' He is a cross between a naughty precocious little boy and a gossip who spreads information regardless as to whether it is true or not.

He plays with himself on the intersex, he wants to copulate like the bunnies and he is just plain and simply adorable. I did of course adopt him although he doesn't know this, he is told that when he has managed to be good for a whole month then we will review his foster status and see about adopting him.

I hope you enjoy reading Timothy's second book 'Community Service' as much as I have enjoyed writing it and as 'The Camel's Dead' which is the first book in this anthology still proves to be popular we are already well underway with the third book which will be called 'Dead Lions to Meet.'

Welcome back to Timothy's diaries. We left him just before Christmas 2016 after he had just managed to conquer the dog-walk although he had to be enticed very slowly over it and was still in fear of the killer seesaw from Nemesis. His diaries continue then as he announces the publication of The Camel's Dead' to anyone who will listen to him. They sell all over the world now and are proving to be very popular but please don't let Timothy know as his head will only get bigger. You could always let me know what you think by leaving a review on Amazon though.

❤

FOREWORD

I first came to know Kathleen in her capacity as a world-class hypnotherapist. At that time I had not yet read her marvelous series of children's books about Life on Belles Haven with unicorns and all manner of magical creatures so I never could have imagined that the heart of a poet beat loudly under her professional exterior.

Our common ground was found through our shared love of animals. Kathleen has devoted decades of her life to rescuing generations of Collie dogs. Her beautiful canine family have not only found a home in 'Love House' and dined like Kings and Queens on 'Steak, Stilton and Carrots Julienne' but, through Kathleen's encouragement and nurture, they have each developed their own unique (and often outrageous) personalities. Their transformation from abandoned, angry, anxious waifs to well adjusted, adoring 'Community Service' luminaries is a testimony to Kathleen's unwavering devotion. She is a marvel!

Kathleen's writing style is as unique as she is. Her writing welcomes you in like an old friend, pours you a drink, settles you by the fire and then takes you on a wild and wonderful ride.

Timothy is a wonderful young man – I wish I could buy him a pie and a pint. He is a rebel and a visionary. He is one of a kind! His diary anthology starting with 'The Camels Dead' and now 'Community Service' and with his third book 'Dead Lions to Meet' well on its way is at times whimsical, poignant, hilarious and thoughtful. I defy anyone not to be enthralled by his escapades.

A book to read all-in-one-go or to dip-in-and-out-of. Or, in my case, to read-all-in-one-go and *then* dip-in-and-out-of. If I ever need a laugh, if I ever need a cry, if I ever need to remind myself that good people who love animals, as I do, still exist – then this book is my 'go-to'. Timothy's diary is a tonic for our modern, stressful lives. Just fabulous!

Clare Molyneux

Playwright and Animal Lover.

Contents.

Jennifer's 1st day at school.
Jennifer the cat.
Timothy's Silver medal day.
Carla Lane fund-raising day.
Patience and a cat.
Jennifer gets Bronze.
The impenetrable Trump wall – escape from Colditz.
Flower child blooms.
The wrong trousers.
Jennifer is a girl.
Silver Lady.
Yes we have no bananas.
Local erections day.
Laddie the Baddie Obituary.
Circle of life.
Laddie the Baddie R.I.P.
Killer see-saw conquered day.
Head boy.
Killer-gate.

I did know what page numbers these were on but somebody added pictures and messed all the numbers up so anyway I have given you the order of the entries in my diaries and I hope you can find them. If not please write to mummy to complain because it wasn't my fault your honour I was busy in the wine cellar trying to sober the judge up when it all went horribly wrong.

I am just letting you all know I have started a new diary now and it is called 'Dead Lions to Meet' so I will look forward to telling you all the gossip I can find as soon as it is ready.
Did you know that rats are neophobic? Well they are you see and we thought we might have one in the chariot so mummy's friend Billy got his big stick out and they had a poke in the chariot to see if there was one but they couldn't find it so they just carried on poking until they were sure and.. oh the lady of the manor is calling so I will have to go as they won't be extending any more dead lions for us and I will be in big trouble again.
Love Timothy. xxxx

Love is a four
legged word.

♥

28th November 2016
Dances with Wolves.

My name is Timothy and I'm a border collie. It has been two weeks since my last confession.

Hello, I'm sorry I've not been on here for a while, I've been quite busy with my illiteratary agent and my publishers. The good news is I will be imprinted on you all within days as my first novel has now been published! It is called 'The Camel's Dead' and is available from Amazon and certain libraries.

So what have I been up to, well let me see now. I have been mostly obedient in the obedience department and only naughty just on the occasions I was caught your honour. I attended my community service last weekend at the training centre and was excellent at being sent away for a lie down and not too bad at all at lining up and looking handsome. When it was time for the torture course I sat with my back to it in protest to show my disgust. I did however do quite well and everybody is nice to me and I get more treats when I do it well so I'm thinking maybe this is a good thing to do after all. I think the lovely Sharon is practicing to be on the Generation Game because when she was enticing me with bribes on the dog-walk on Sunday I was lured by a piece of sausage, then a piece of dog meal, then a piece of gravy bone followed by a piece of pie and I'm sure the last bribe was a piece of fluff but I think mummy was just hoping that the cuddly toy and the colour television didn't appear. Ethan who is also owned by Luna said he would give me a special cuddle and two sausages if I did the dog-walk and when I went for the cuddles he whispered in my ear 'Just wait conehead, I will arrange it so we can have special private lessons because I have The Power' I just smiled sweetly and ate my sausages.

So anyway after such a busy week editing my book with my ghost writers and then meetings meetings meetings I was reminded by the mummy that it was time for my community service and so we did go. Freya has to do an hour first but she's not as naughty as me she just does the one hour every week whereas hunky little me has to do two hours!

So Freya goes in first and she tells me that she was dead boss like but I have been excused and can go home.

Apparently Brian who lives in an old peoples home and has been naughty and has been told by Matron he has to be back by one-o-clock, he said however because I am a superstar adored by millions and a legend in my own mind that I can come in and just do the torture course. How could I refuse such an offer? That was a rectal question by the way. So there I was in my own private lesson and I quite liked this it reminded me of my special lessons with Andrea so I went like this I went 'Oh go on then Brian just to make you happy I'll do it' and so I did and Brian forgot I needed gently enticing across the dog-walk and he walked quite fast so I had to walk quite fast myself to catch the enticement and I did it twice your honour and was so cool mummy's mouth wouldn't shut.

So anyway we said thank you and we were all going home when Luna the white wolf turns up, Luna owns Lynne and Ethan remember and she said I should stay for some fun. So Ethan, do you remember I told you we had special cuddles last Sunday? Yes well that same Ethan decided to train me and so I jumped jumps and we played hide and seek in the long tunnel and I did the A-frame and go on, guess what?

Go on, just guess. Well so you see it's like this your honour. After the wobbly wood training worked and I realised that it was ok for wood to touch my dainty feet and it wouldn't kill me then mummy and Sharon have been tempting and enticing me with bribes ever so slowly over the dog-walk and it has been working. On my private lesson with Brian, you know the one who lives in an old peoples home, and I think he is owned by Pauline, well you see he didn't entice me slowly he enticed me more quickly and so I did move more quickly to follow the enticement. So, when Ethan come along for my second private lesson of the day he enticed me even more quickly and so I had to move even more quickly over the dog-walk to get my treat! I know you're not going to believe this but guess what? I can RUN over the dog-walk like a BOSS! After a while Luna got fed up with her Ethan training me so she joined in and she snook up to me on the dog-walk and told me to hurry up and pushed me so I went like this I went "ok great white wolf, I will move more quickly just for you" and so I did. Then Luna sent for her brothers and when they came in it was fun and I danced with wolves until mummy said we had to go home. We didn't let Freya back in in case she thought I might need protecting from said wolves your honour.

The next day was Sunday and Sharon had seen the video evidence of me running across the dog-walk and she was so pleased with me and so I did it again and I did lots of jumps too and everyone was pleased.

I am a little concerned about the conversation mummy had with Sharon before we left to go home. Sharon told mummy that she has been playing on a seesaw with Brian [you know the one who is owned by Pauline but she keeps him in an old peoples home for safe keeping.] and they have been bouncing up and down on tyres....

I will write again as soon as I know more.
Love Timothy xxxx

My name is Timothy Conehead the Invincible and I'm a border
collie. It has been three days since my last confession and I'm
Devvoed, just devvoed.

So you see there I was all excited and ready to go hunting with
Freya the Hunter and as I approached the wobbly wood training
area I stopped dead in my tracks. Not exactly dead I was still
breathing your honour but I was prostrated and couldn't move. The
killer seesaw with murderous tendencies who is currently
handcuffed to the ground at the torture course in Formby has sent
his cousin to stalk me! There he was lying in wait for me, half
covering the wobbly wood I had long since made friends with and
just waiting to attack me with it's deathly noise as I crossed it.
I sent out a quick request to the SAS to be airlifted out but mummy
did block this request and I was just devvoed.

Mummy did come to me and she saw I was sad and she went like
this she went " Come here Timothy while I have a word in your
shell like" mummy can be very perssertive when she wants to be,
especially with me very perssertive indeed. and then she went "
Look into my eyes Timothy and listen to what I have to say to
you" So I did your honour. Then she went " Timothy, sometimes
in life things come along and they upset us, sometimes they
frighten us or make us angry or sad or any kind of negative
emotion and it's not nice." then she went "Now we can either let
them upset us for the rest of our lives so they leave us bitter and
sad or we can conquer them so we can become better and glad. Do
you understand Timothy?" I didn't but I just smiled in a handsome
way. Then she went "So we are going to decapitate you completely
over the next few weeks and it will lift you over these fears." I just
closed my eyes and I did think "Oh yes, there is a God, mummy is
going to lift me over the wobbly metal sheet cousin of the
aforementioned Killer seesaw." Then I heard a bloodcurdling
wonky metal banging noise and I opened my eyes. I nearly fainted
again, mummy Freya and Baddie were all over the other side of the

homicidal wobbly metal cousin. My heart stopped beating, it was broken! It didn't really your honour but it just sounds good for the story. Mummy smiled at me which makes a change as she mostly gives me those "Do as I say now or die!" looks. I was just so scared your honour. I touched the metal offender with my delicate dainty foot and it made a horrible noise. "That's it" I thought " I'm never going to be able to go out hunting ever again forever and as long as I live."

Mummy smiled again and I thought to myself " I wonder if mummy has received any plain brown paper parcels recently from our postman, the one who likes me because I am handsome."

Just then I noticed she had a sausage in her hand, a big fat meaty one, no not the sort that would come in a brown paper parcel delivered by the postman but the type you would find in Aldi in the 'Bribes & Enticements' range. In my haste to be bribed by the sausage I manged to escape death and with great speed found myself next to mummy and relieved her of the said sausage!.

"That wasn't so bad now, was it Conehead?" she smiled. Then she went "Now just keep your pecker up Timothy but don't play with it." She smiled again, "Something is definitely going on with all these smiles, I thought to myself and although I didn't agree with her I smiled sweetly and we went hunting.

I will update you as soon as I can.

Love Timothy. xxxx

P.S. I think my aunty Pauline might be in league with the killer seesaw and I think she might have let it's cousin in while we were all out. I'm sure I am right your honour because she left some supplies for us poorly fed dogs along with a note that said 'Sorry' just sat on the doorstep for when we got home....

Friday 2nd December 2016
Timothy is a phenomena.

My name is Timothy Conehead the Invincible and I'm a border collie. It has been only a day since my last confession.

Listen, listen I'm so excited! Our Freya has just told me that I'm a pherenomea and I am an overnight sensation in a few weeks time. Freya who is a girl of course so therefore knows more than me, says that I am a trendsetter too and that everyone is talking about my extra marital training aids and that soon every garden in the land will have Timothy Conehead Cones and Special Edition Timothy Conehead wobbly pink training planks and also wobbly killer metal training planks too. She says there are factories all over the land gearing up for the pherenomea that is "Timothy Conehead the Invincible"

I'm not sure if she is telling the truth though because Laddie the Baddie is rolling his eyes all around the room and Freya has a silly smile on her face, a bit like mummy's silly smile..
If anyone wants mine they can just have them for free.

Anyway I have to go to bed early tonight because mummy says I am going to be tyred tomorrow and she still has that strange smile on her face. I wonder if she has spent too much time in the herb cellar again.
I will report in again soon.

Love Timothy xxxx

Sunday 4th December 2016
Dogs in Space.

My name is Timothy Conehead the Invincible and I'm a border collie. It has been a few days since my last confession. It's bad news I'm afraid, very bad news, the killer seesaw has been patrolled for good behavior.

Oh it's just dreadful news your honour, dreadful. I arrived for my community service on Saturday only to find the killer see-saw with murderous tendencies had been released from its confinement and furthermore it had been given a dog bed to aid it in it's evil bid to trap me.

To be fair your honour it had initially been fitted with a tyre as a rubber silencer which could have worked only Shayla got carried away on it and thought it was a trampoline, I think they should have left the tyre where it was, 'Dogs in Space' has a good ring to it for a book or a film and we could have all been featured in the next John Lewis Christmas advert.

Mummy says decapitation will continue for at least the next six months because that's how long my community service is to last for. I'm just abbreviated and dismal but mummy says I will be glad in the end that we didn't give up. How does she know I'll be glad? Is she Mystic Meg? I'm here to tell you I will be happy to give up right here and now your honour, right this very minute!

Actually I've just been having a think. If I give up now I wont get to see the lovely friends I've made like Ethan and I won't get to dance with wolves or upset Brian or anything and I think I might miss lining up and looking handsome for Sharon and doing a 'down' for an hour with my aunty Rita. Oh well I'll just have to keep my paws crossed and hope decapitation isn't too painful.

I just heard mummy talking to someone on the phone and she went like this she went " I'm going to drug the boy, I'll use that fresh stuff in the herb cellar, no one will know" Please don't tell her I told you.

I will write again soon,
Love Timothy. xxxx

December 8th 2016
36th anniversary of John Lennon's murder.
Timothy's Recipe Book.

My name is Timothy Conehead the Invincible and I'm a border collie. It has been three days since my last confession. I don't think Becky is speaking to mummy.

So you see it's like this, I have a big sister and she is called Becky amongst other things and she comes to stay with us sometimes for the weekend, So this was her weekend and she came to me and she said "Hello handsome Timothy, you are even more handsome than you were last time," I knew she was right and I just smiled sweetly. Then she went "Is it true you have published your diaries Timothy? Can I read them please?" So I thought about it for a minute and then I went like this, I went "Oh beautiful sister who is adorable, did you bring me any sweeties?" The Becky lifted up a big bag of goodies in response. "Of course you can read my book, don't say anything to the mummy though she thinks it is full of recipes."

And so my beautiful big sister Becky who is lovely and kind to me and brings me sweeties did settle down to read my book. Every so often she would look up at mummy and just look at her and shake her head and then she would read some more. Laddie and Freya and handsome little me giggled secretly.

After a while she went like this she just went "I didn't know you had a flamingo mummy?"

After another while she went "Where on earth did you buy a camel from?"

After a third little while she went "Mummy, I thought you had promised to stop growing herbs in the cellar after your last conviction?

Mummy looked at my big sister Becky in a confused way

[mummy often looks confused though, we think it has something to do with being owned and part owned by so many border collies over the years] so she is looking at Becky in a confused way and then she goes like this she goes " What are you reading oh daughter of mine?" and Becky looks at me and she goes "Oh wonderful mummy I am only reading Timothy's recipe book, he seems to use an awful lot of herbs in his cooking" and then she looked at me again and smiled.

Mummy just sat there for a little while and then she went " I must have a read of Timothy's book myself, lots of people are reading it I believe and I've noticed people smiling at me in a strange way once they have started it."

Mummy went to do some gardening in the cellar for a rest and when she came back she looked at me with the instant death stare and she went like this. " Conehead tell me you haven't been telling people about my private life in your recipe book" So what could I say? I decided to be obedient and I went 'Of course I haven't been telling people about your private life in my recipe book oh amazing mummy" That's what she asked me to say, wasn't it? Then I just slunk away

I'll let you know of any further developments.

Love Timothy. xxxx

Sunday 11th December 2016
Whiter Shade of Pale.

My name is Timothy Conehead the Invincible and I'm a border collie it has been three days since my last confession and somebody has grassed me up!!

Hello, I've been grassed up your honour and it was probably one of those woolly backs.

Mummy keeps getting texts to ask how much she is selling her herbs for, I think people want to stock up for Christmas and she is not well pleased your honour, she is not a bit well pleased at all.

Does anyone know the market price for marjoram and coriander please?

Anyway I had to do my community service again this week and most of it did pass without major incident your honour, Sharon who just thinks I'm adorable thought I was particularly adorable this week and was enjoying our cuddles so much she decided to roll around on the floor hugging and kissing me for ten minutes. Everyone else was jealous I could tell, some of them were crying they were so jealous. I think they were crying anyway. Then she was asking mummy when were the booze liners due back in and did she have any tips she could share with her. I hope Sharon doesn't end up getting arrested too.

On the way out Brian came to me and he was on his knees begging, it wasn't a pretty sight, he went like this he went 'Oh wise and wonderful Timothy please don't write anything bad about me this week or I'll have to get my friend Sconehead to come and sort you out' so I went like this I went 'Calm down, Brian calm down Brian and keep your shirt on oh wonderful trainer, you know Matron has told you not to get excited I will promise not to write anything bad about you for just this one week but I can promise no more and I'll have you know that your mate Sconehead is my cousin' Brian went a whiter shade of pale and then he went 'Thank

you Timothy I am so grateful is there nothing you are afraid of?'
I hesitated in a bewildered way and then I went like this, I went
'There is only one thing on this earth that frightens me Brian and
that is killer seesaws! I have written my letter to Santa Claus to
ask for a friendly one, if I can conquer this I can conquer the
world!'

My Aunty Rita came and brought me some sweeties and so I
signed my new recipe book for her. I'm hoping mummy doesn't get
into the mood for cooking over Christmas or I could be in a spot of
trouble.

On Sunday Sharon was awol and I'm wondering if she had gone in
search of some Booze Liners. Anyway so anyway Pauline had put
Brian back in the old peoples home for safekeeping as he was
complaining of creaky bones but then she had to ask Matron if she
could borrow him back again for a couple of hours so I could do
training with my friends Shayla, Jess and Digby and all the others
on community service. Matron said he had to be back for two o
clock though for his medicine and his enigma for his guts.

Brian was really, really nice to me. I think he might be scared of
me now and anyway guess what? Go on Guess? I did the wooden
seesaw for him just because he was so nice to me, I'm not sure
whether I want to do it again but I did do it! Maybe my friend
Ethan who is owned by Luna could help me next time. I then
proceeded in an orderly fashion and did jump all the jumps on my
own and sat on the green box at the end all by myself while
mummy was still stood at the first jump with her gob open in the
OMG style.

I'll write again soon. Xx
Love Timothy. xxxx

Wednesday 21st December 2016

Yule.

The shortest day of the year.

Polishing Act.

My name is Timothy Conehead the Invincible and I'm a border collie. It has been over a week since mt last confession and I need your help please.

Hello,

Does anyone know where the rest of the aerosol can has gone from the furniture polish please? I don't know where it is you see and mummy is blaming me. The only piece of discriminating evidence your honour is the plastic top that was discovered next to me this morning and appears to have teeth marks on it.

I have contacted MI5 but they are apparently too busy now until the New Year.

I have of course denied all knowledge of the aforementioned polish, mummy doesn't bring it out very often you see but because Christmas is looming she felt that she should remove a few inches of the dust and polish the furniture up. She's not very happy. I heard her talking to her friend and she went like this she went 'I'm not very flocking happy with these collies, they were supposed to polish everything while I was at work and now they are denying all knowledge of the whereabouts of the can and I've got at least six inches to shift and that's before I have to start on the judge in the basement! I'm just not very flocking happy at all!'

We think that somebody broke in and took the metal part of the polish just simply to frame me your honour. I suspect they are jealous of my handsome physique.

Your help in this matter would be greatly appreciated as I have been threatened with being shoved up a gumtree if it doesn't appear soon.

.

If you could also keep your eyes open also for a dolly shoe, a glove, half a packet of biscuits and a special Christmas ornament that seems to have disappeared too please. We think the burglar must have been an double amputee who was addicted to polish fumes who had the munchies your honour and just wanted a bit of Christmas cheer.

I will write soon and let you know if they turn up.

Love Timothy xxxx

Christmas Eve.

The Night Before Christmas.

Twas the night before Christmas and the mummy was stressed,
The turkey was naked, the tree wasn't dressed,
The mulled wine was inviting and so was the port,
"I'll just have a wee dram of each" mummy thought,
So she poured the drink out and gathered us near,
We all sat around, mummy dabbed at a tear,
Tonight we will talk about all those who have passed,
So we did but we kept Sir Lord Jack to the last,
Sir Lord Jack was just so very special you see,
He smiles from a bauble now on our Christmas tree,
We talked about each border collie in turn,
How we all came to mummy to love and to learn,
That life is not all about suffering, pain and neglect,
It's all about Love and learning to correct,
Those bad habits we learned in the days gone by,
There's nothing you can't change unless you don't try,
Even trust when you've become full of aggression,
With love and kindness you'll lift the oppression,
And learn that not everyone is cruel and mean,
If you're lucky mummy will allow you to clean,
The dishes and pans and even the moat,
It's fun living here and you'll get a red coat,
With matching red collar, lead, tag and bow,
You'll support Liverpool or you'll just have to go,
Christmas time is so special and all about love,
It's about peace and forgiveness sent from above,
We are all made of energy, none of us die,
We just drift away while our loved ones cry,
While we are here we must learn how to respect,
Each other in turn as no one is perfect,
If you focus on Love, keep your heart and mind pure,
You'll be happier here and feel more secure,

If you're greedy and mean and put people down,
You'll never be happy never not deep down,
So this night before Christmas lets all stop and think,
We can all learn to love even those on the brink,
So with love in your hearts your words and your deeds,
Give thanks for your achievements and meeting your needs,
Lets all raise a glass and toast those we love,
Who can't be with us now but watch from above,
Merry Christmas to all Merry Christmas to you,
May love and peace in your life shine through.

Love Timothy Conehead the Invincible. Xxxx

My name is Timothy Conehead the Invincible and it has been a
few hours since my last confession. Merry Christmas everyone.

Hello,

Mummy says a lot of people have forgotten what Christmas is
about, they think it is just about presents and tinsel and turkey and
it is but it's also about remembering the message that came when
Jesus was born in Bethlehem, in a stable just like the ones at our
local horse sanctuary Shy Lowen. Mummy says that it happened
such a long time ago and that Jesus might not have been born on
25th December just like Sir Lord Jack might not have been born on
11th June like Gene Wilder and I might not have been born on 18th
June like Sir Macca of Beatleland. Sometimes when people don't
actually know the right date then they just pick one and stick to it.
Celebrations for the winter solstice happened long before Jesus
was born and it is always late December that is probably why
December 25th was chosen as His special day.

Anyway so Mummy says that everyone knows that the Hippies
were right and that 'All you need is Love' and she says it is
important to remember that Jesus was the first real Hippie and if
we could just all understand that we need to be kind to each other
and forgive people when they get things wrong, especially me and
if we all just did one kind deed a day and no bad ones then there
would be happier people all over the place and everywhere. He
said that you mustn't lead people into temptation and that means it
wasn't my fault that I ate the Stilton erm except that we are not
supposed to take things that don't belong to us either. We really
like Jesus because he could turn water unto wine and he wasn't
overly keen on the tax collector, something to be admired your
honour. He believed in the power of the mind and the power of
belief and he believed in miracles and helping people. He believed
in being kind and helping the homeless and the poor people and

hungry and thirsty ones too. He believed in doing small things with great love. Jesus was a very kind man and we want to wish him Happy Birthday and a Merry Christmas to everyone.

Love from Timothy xxxx

P.S. It is ok to be a reindeer but it is not ok to bully a reindeer because he has a red nose. It is ok to not agree with other peoples religions or beliefs but it is not ok to be nasty about it. It is not ok to be nasty about anything. It is ok to be an atheist but it is not ok to shame religions and spirituality as silly or not real. It is not ok in the name of religion or for any other reason to be homophobic, misogynistic, racist or hateful in any way to other people. Being hateful is unkind. If you insist on being hateful or unkind then please keep it to yourself or post it on your own wall. It is of course ok to be a unicorn. All you need is Love. Peace & Love and a very Merry Christmas to all and whatever He is to you may your God go with you. ☮❤

My name is Timothy Conehead the Invincible and I'm a border
collie. It has been just one day since my last confession and I
might just be in trouble.

Hello,
Mummy might be logging on tonight, I heard her talking on the
phone to her friend. Not the imaginary one I told you about, the
other one. Anyway so anyway I'm going to post a recipe to keep
her away from my diary your honour.

Today's recipe is:-
As I am sure all of you are sick of the sight or turkey already, I
have prepared for you with no expense spared a delectable recipe
for you to feast your eyes on and then your belly. I give you:-

Camel Burgers.

Firstly one must visit the cellar in search of the camel that is
lurking there, you may have a little trouble catching it as it has
become quite anxious and nervous since meeting me and usually
lurks in dark corners hoping to evade capture.

Once one has the said camel one must now pass it through the
mincer thirteen times, this may prove difficult to begin with but do
persist because after you've got to thirteen it should be more
compliable.

Eggs.
Eggs are a good binding agent and as our camel is fed on bread and
water like us poorly fed dogs then his motions really do need
binding.
You can go to the supermarket for these eggs or you can be lucky
like me and find some in a neighbours garden that has chickens

running around, not the headless ones though these tend to be too runny, a bit like the camels motion really.

Mushrooms.
Collect two small mushrooms from the mushroom cellar, now be very careful as these are magic mushrooms and very powerful so take two small ones only. If you use more than two you might not live to regret it.

From the machete cupboard please select the smallest one to dice said mushrooms and add to the mix.

Take a trip to the herb cellar being careful to not breathe too deeply and you will find an array of illegal herbs. The marjoram is the most pungent and should be handled with great care.

Do NOT touch anything labelled £.s.d. This will incur a heavy sentence should the judge catch you but if you're really quiet you won't wake him as he will have coma toes and be intoxicated in the corner near where you found the camel.

Flour.
Flour is a fine white powder. This is your missing ingredient and being very careful to select the correct white powder, add this to your mix.

You need to find a friend called Patty to help with the mixing and she will know the right shape to mould these succulent burgers to.

Cooking the Camel Burger.

We find the best way to cook the camel burger is in a frying pan, so making sure you have licked it clean after your last masterpiece add a little special marjoram oil and then add your burgers and cook slowly.

When they are cooked you can serve them in bed on a bun and don't worry of you get the munchies as you have enough burgers for a couple of weeks at least.

Lettuce.
Now you might want to add a garnish of lettuce unfortunately this could prove impossible if you have rampant rabbits and copulating bunnies like we do as the are a flocking nuisance and eat it all as soon as it grows. You could chance the luminous lettuce from the herb cellar but only if you don't mind glowing in the dark.

To accompany your sumptuous camel burger I suggest a visit to the wine cellar being careful not to disturb the judge, mummy will give him a good seeing to later when she comes round. As this is a red meat may I suggest a cheeky little Shiraz or a charming mellow Merlot. Do NOT under any circumstances touch mummy's special reserve vintage port, this is purely to accompany her steak and Stilton, mummy is required to have Stilton for medicinal purposes on a regular basis so she has this for dinner every night.

I hope you've enjoyed our recipe of the day and don't forget you can subscribe for more delightful recipes on Facebook at Timothy Conehead the Invincible!

I'm just off to check that the judge is still breathing.

I not sure mummy will be logging on tonight after all, she's laying coma toes under the Christmas tree. She served s special brandy flavoured Christmas pudding for dessert but when she opened it this morning she said it didn't seem to have enough brandy so she soaked it in a pint of brandy for four hours. I suspect there wasn't enough Christmas pudding in the brandy. My big sister Becky doesn't mind it means she can watch whatever she wants on the TV without mummy giving the death stare....

I will write again as soon as I can,
Merry Christmas everyone.

Love Timothy. xxxx

Saturday31st December 2016
New Years Eve.
Caring & Sharing.

My name is Timothy and I'm a border collie and it has been a week
since my last confession and I don't know where mummy has
hidden the port.

Hello everyone,
I'm not sure if I have been repelled from torture training or not
your honour, mummy said I had six months of community service
left to do. I wonder if Sharon has heard that I can do a reverse
finish like a boss and she has patrolled me for good behaviour? I
just know that I haven't been there for ages and ages and months
since a week before Christmas.

Did you get any nice things from Santa Claus? I wrote to him and
asked for a friendly seesaw but it hasn't arrived yet. We got lots of
stuff but we killed most of it quickly to be fair, just in case they
had any ideas about taking over or anything. Mummy got lots of
nice things too, there was a nice balance of unicorns, border collies
and port really and some of the port came with my name on too! I
can't find it though, mummy has hidden it away from me.

We were out bunny hunting yesterday and I met my mate Ben, you
know the one who owns Wendy along with his sister Ruby. Well
Ben is my hero you see because he can do everything and is top of
the class is torture training and isn't afraid of killer seesaws or
anything. Anyway so anyway I feel really sorry for him now
because all he got for Christmas is a piece of string, isn't that
terrible? Just a piece of string. I've told him it will be ok and that
when the booze liners are in next time I will get mummy to let his
Wendy know so she can make a little couple of bob extra for next
Christmas too.
So anyway I have told Ben that I will bring him a piece of my
reindeer for him to play with and Laddie says he can have his
snowman's head and our Freya said she thinks she might still have
a leg left off Santa and if she can find it then she will bring it out

just for Ben.
I will write again soon.
Love Timothy. xxxx

Hello my name is Timothy and I'm a border collie it has been one day since my last confession and I have terrible news for you.

Well you see it's like this, the virgins are still on strike and I'm not sure if its because mummy hasn't paid the bill or not and it could be and I'm not sure if Wendy has either. Anyway so anyway there we were out on our morning hunt and I was a boss doing my reverse finish for June, well it wasn't exactly for June it was for a treat your honour but I let her think it was just for her so anyway.

Where was I then? I have been regressed again by one of you wools, who was it this time? Anyway we were all being good and looking handsome in a begging sort of way and waiting for June to give us some treats because none of us have been fed for days and when we looked around mummy and Wendy had gone, they were nowhere to be seen and nobody knows where they are, have you seen them? We are afraid they may have been adopted by a passing alien ship and I'm not sure if they were wearing clean underwear or anything.

Oh it's just terrible news, apparently Wendy has got 4G and mummy only has 3G and anyway because of this it means Wendy picked up the signal from a passing booze ship and they've both gone to see if they can earn a little extra couple of bob. We don't know when they will be back your honour. They were going to let Sharon know but the virgin disappeared again so they've put her name down for the next one.

I've got to get back home soon too because someone needs to feed the dead camel in the basement and I have to check on the judge to see if he is ready for another good seeing to again for when mummy returns but we can't go home yet because June won't let us.

Please help, June is doing a Sir Ken Dodd trick and keeping us all hostage and she won't let us go home on our own. She says mummy and Wendy are up to no good and until they have returned and paid June for her babysitting duties then we have to stay with her.
I am enclosing exhibit A your honour, this clearly shows that we have all been abandoned and are begging June to let us go home.

I will update you as soon as I can.
Love Timothy xxxx

June with her hostages..

Monday 2nd January 2017
The Invincibles.

My name is Timothy Conehead the Invincible and I'm a border collie. It has only been one day since my last confession and I have a complaint your honour.

Hello, It has come to my attention your honour that there is some infiltrating going on by an infiltrator and it has to stop!
You may remember yesterday that we were kidnapped by the lovely June and held hostage for hours and hours while Wendy and mummy were on the game or something and we got so hungry that I unscrewed Junes leg so we could eat and so anyway we eventually escaped and we hid in the cellar with the dead camel and waited to see what time mummy would eventually come home. It was really cold down there but our bread and water had been left out so I managed to make us some herb butties and so we did have a laugh until we fell asleep. We are not sure what we were laughing at but it was very funny your honour.

Anyway so anyway before I fell asleep I kept logging on, I keep a spare iPad down there you see and I noticed that somebody was looking for the key to the herb cellar and the mummy, whatever game she was playing said he could have one! Well your honour I am shocked and disappointed and I am here to tell you that the only men allowed to have a key to the cellar are Sir Lord Jack who is down here sometimes but he doesn't need a key anymore because he can teleport and handsome little me, Laddie and my mate Ben! – oh oh I nearly forgot! The judge is allowed down here because we need to keep him happy just in case mummy gets arrested again.
Mummy has been reprimanded severely or she will be when she has sobered up enough to understand what I am saying to her.
I will write again soon and let you know what happens,
Love Timothy. xxxx

P.S. I am enclosing exhibit A your honour which shows clearly my pack with our women. In order this is Laddie the baddie who to be fair is a bit past it but not giving up yet and can still pack a punch when he wants to, next is Princess Freya the bunny slayer she is my concubine but only when she is in the mood, next comes the very beautiful Shayla she is the number one pinup girl for Germans everywhere, next we have the gorgeous sexy handsome chap adored by millions and a legend in his own mind, I give you Timothy Conehead the Invincible who is handsome little me in case you didn't realise, next is Ruby who is a feisty little girl who likes to shout at us all especially on a Tuesday, next is Ben he's not a flower pot man but he does like a little weed now and then. Missing from the picture of our gang this year is Sir Lord Jack who will always be with us in spirit and Moody Misty who is currently on bed rest, we think Laddie gave her a black eye when no one was looking. We are known locally by many different names but we are using our stage name today and we are - "The Invincibles."

The
Invincibles..

Monday 16th January 2017
Blue Monday.
Cold Turkey.

My name is Timothy and I'm a border collie and it has been at
least two weeks since my last confession and it's bad news I'm
afraid.

Oh it's dreadful news, I haven't been repelled or patrolled at all and
I had to go back to torture training last week. Apparently the
trainers needed a break from me and I have to do my community
service now until my birthday in June at least. If I haven't made
friends with the killer seesaw from Nemesis by then I will be given
away to the highest bidder.

On my first day back it was Junes birthday, remember she is
owned by Shayla and Misty and we all sang happy birthday to her
to June that is, not Shayla and Misty. Wendy held the lovely
chocolate cake as we all sang to June. . I say lovely chocolate cake
but I only got a tiny bit your honour because Angela who is owned
by Ruby and Lily only let me have a quick lick and then she went
like this, she went ' Push off Timothy, I don't care even if you spit
on it I am still eating it Oh Legendary one now do one or else!' I
wasn't sure quite what she wanted me to do your honour but she
looked like she meant business and as she comes from a very
rough part of town I decided to back away quietly.

I did try the seesaw in my advanced class the following Saturday
and I was just so scared but it didn't attack me or anything when I
wasn't looking and Ethan and Sharon helped me with some
chicken so it wasn't all bad your honour. My aunty Rita gave me a
hug when she heard and said I was very brave and dead clever
when I showed her my reverse finish.

I was really splendid in a marvellously handsome way in the
obedience part of the advanced class, I was on my very best
behaviour having slipped Helga a special little something from the
herb cellar earlier. I gave the rest of the class some too but Helga

had the most. It was really funny in an amusing way as there I was looking gorgeously handsome in a stunning kind of way and exceptionally obedient and one after the other the rest of the class was naughty! I just sat there looking innocent which of course I was as I didn't make them take it.

So anyway where was I? Oh yes Sharon. Sharon is the boss you see and Sharon knows everything there is to know about dog training, even killer see-saw decapitation training. Sharon is owned by Wilma and Helga, now Wilma is a goody two shoes and didn't want any of the special treats I brought with me from the herb cellar but of course Helga had loads. The thing is you see because Sharon is the boss nobody questions anything and we all just do as she says, if Sharon says jump that is what we do.

Anyway so anyway Helga decided to rebel and even though she is normally perfect in a quintessential sort of way she refused to do as she was told, it was so funny. We don't think Sharon thought it was funny though especially when Helga kept answering back but we were all quietly giggling but only when Sharon wasn't looking your honour. I hope Helga found the cold turkey I slipped into her crate for her.

The following day and for the first time in the history of mankind I did the entire course [minus anything with killer in it's name] all on my own and without running off or refusing or anything your honour. I think I might be getting the hang of it now as I can see my friends seem to be enjoying the torture training so maybe I will too one day. Mummy says stranger things have happened.

Anyway so anyway I'm sorry it has been such a long time since my last confession. I'm not sure if mummy has been lying under a weatherman or been run down by something when she wasn't looking but every time I have come to write up my secret diaries she has been playing games with herself on the intersex and I'm sure it's not good for her.

I will make her eat lots of our home-made chicken soup with extra herbs so as she feels better soon and I can write more often, I have a secret to tell you about Wendy and June but I can't say anything yet your honour I can hear mummy on her way back up from the wine cellar, she is making a port-wine jus to go with tonight's steak and stilton. I do hope I manage to get a drop or two, she is bound to leave some in the pan and it's my turn to lick the dishes clean tonight. Yummy..

I will write as soon as I can.

Love Timothy. Xxxx

My name is Timothy and I'm a border collie it has only been three days since my last confession and I'm just rushed off my feet nursing again.

Hello,
It's like this you see, our Laddie the Baddie has been up to no good again and spending too much time in the wine cellar and now he has gone and got wobbly head syndrome or being drunk in the vestibule sickness again. Wendy, who is our paramedic on standby had to be called in on an emergency basis on Tuesday to help mummy load our old codger into the Chariot. She is on a zero hours contract with no pay to be reviewed in 2020.

So anyway he was rushed at 90 miles an hour to see Mr Dunn and we were all so worried because he couldn't even walk or anything but by the time he got there he had perked up a bit and was trying to get sausage out of mummy's pocket. Mummy has been so worried and thought Baddie might be joining Sir Lord Jack for a rest from all of us but Mr Dunn said no, it wasn't his time to go and he had to stay to annoy us for a while longer. He gave him a big needle and some morning sickness pills, Freya says I'm thick and as soon as she has learnt how to use the keyboard like what I can then she is going to takeover in a bid to bring some sense to my witterings. Oh I see, he gave our Laddie some anti-sickness pills. Silly me.

Laddie didn't eat very much on the Tuesday but he was led into temptation by some steak and Stilton on Wednesday and has now been officially put on the 'Fine Dining Menu' list. He wasn't allowed any port as mummy thought he was already drunk enough. So it is only me and Freya who are the poorly fed dogs now but we don't mind as it means we will get to smell all the wondrous delicacies that mummy will cook for him like braised steak with carrots julienne and smoked haddock with asparagus, Aberdeen Angus mince, rack of lamb, sardines and smoked salmon oh my mouth is watering just thinking about all the lovely smells we will get to smell. We might even be lucky and get some leftovers to go with our bread and water.

Anyway so anyway, mummy didn't read the small print when our lovely auntie Pauline gave mummy the wobbly metal plank and it has to go back. I was really pleased to hear this piece of information your honour as I am not overly fond of it to be honest but now sadly I have heard that mummy Wendy and June are going to be in the missionary position with the judge and, oh sorry I may have that wrong. They are going on a secret mission with the judge and a metal plank may or may not be involved. I will let you know when I have more inside information. Does anyone know what a pimp is please..?

Laddie says thank you for all the Love, hugs and prayers and get well wishes and promises to be causing trouble somewhere as soon as he can.

Love and hugs too for some of my school mates, Misty who is recovering well and now also the lovely sweet Wilma who has broken her leg and my big special friend Luna who has a bad problem with her tummy. Hope you are all fit and well soon.

I will keep you updated on the proceedings as soon as I can.
Love Timothy xxxx

Friday 20th January 2017
Winner Takes it All.

My name is Timothy Conehead the Invincible and I'm a border collie and I have an extra confession to make. I'm in big trouble again.

Hello everyone,
You see it was like this your honour I was so happy that my new novel 'The Camel's Dead' full of mystery intrigue and lies, lies and more lies innuendo and sleaze is selling so well and then I remembered that I had run this competition to win one of my books only you see it was me who was supposed to make the draw.

So anyway I forgot. I have just been so busy you see with my agent and my publishers and did you know you can borrow my book from Liverpool Central Libraries? Well you can so there and well so you see I have just been away with the fairies and basking in the glory of being such a legend in my own mind and now I've been told off.

So without further ado and only six weeks late we have made the draw!

We wrote all the names out and put them on the floor and then got our Laddie the Baddie to walk around and the first one he put his nose on was the winner. I hope the winner didn't mind Laddie putting his nose on them.

Would you like me to tell you who it was?

Oh go on then and the winner is.... Elliot Shaw who will be notified forthwith and straightaway.

If anyone would like to buy a copy they are on sale from Amazon either kindle or paperback. You can also buy them direct from mummy who is Kathleen Phythian who can be messaged in the messenger message box. Love Timothy. xxxx

Friday 20th January 2017
International Fart Day

My name is Timothy Conehead the Invincible and I'm a border collie, it has only been a short while since my last confession and I just need to fart.

Hello,

Am I allowed to say fart? I know I can say trump but is fart allowed your honour? We've all been trumping all day long, we had beans for breakfast you see and now all we can do is trump, trump, trump, trump, trump. Our Laddie trumped that much that he ended up with diarrhoea and we had to get some more medicine for him. He's still trumping though. Mummy says that the big trump is so full of diarrhoea and gas that the world could end up exploding.

Anyway so anyway we have to focus on the positive or else we have to do six months in the naughty drawer with no food or drugs or anything so we will try to forget about the nasty pong and think about all the good things in the world like torture training and having fun in the polygamy tunnel.

Laddie the Baddie continues to improve your honour and now his tummy has settled down he has just had a fine dining experience of steamed chicken breast served on a bed of basmati rice, he has not quite sobered up yet but mummy and Mr Dunn are hopeful that he will soon.

I will report back in as soon as I have any news for you.

Love Timothy xxxx.

Saturday 21st January 2017
International Conepetition Games.

Oh it just gets worse your honour, after all the farting around
yesterday – did we decide whether it was alright for me to say fart?
So it was like this you see, when we got to training we found that
Sharon was awol and apparently working somewhere else, we are
mot sure whether she was working the cruise liners or not I think I
need to look into it.

So there we were and Matron had decided she needed a rest from
Brian so she had let him out for the day which was probably a
good thing really and Pauline who owns him said he had to work
with us or else.

Well anyway there I was looking handsome and very dashing
when Brian decided we were going to play a game, he said he was
going to play a game with Conehead but mummy objected and so
he used plastic cones instead. Ethan who was training Pirate Leo
today because Luna who owns him and Lynn was still swinging
the lead on her sick bed, well that Ethan decided to call it a
'conepetition' and so there we were and we had to sit nicely for a
few moments at the first cone and then we were each called in turn
and we were meant to stop at the middle cone. Well Shayla who is
a pin-up girl for all the Germans and also one of my girlfriends
was amazing and she was awarded the Gold medal for placing her
bum down nearest the middle cone for a sausage, then came the
gorgeous handsome one, that's me in case you didn't guess and I
got awarded the Silver medal and shared a joint with Monty who is
also a border collie and then the gorgeous Poppy got the Bronze
medal. Pirate Leo who is blind deaf and not so dumb took all the
medals in the paraplegic section and there has been a warrant
issued for his arrest.

I was perfect at being sent away for a lie down and then sitting up
again and excellent in the follow the treat exercise, our Freya tells
me that she is almost as good as me now so I might have to lace
her water with something special to slow her down again. Anyway

so there I was thinking it must be home-time soon and Brian, the one who has been let out of the nursing home for the day – yes that one well he goes like this he goes 'Come on Conehead, do you fancy a go on the big boys agility course?' I went like this I went 'No it's ok Brian I'll just pop off home now if that's ok with you' but then he did a really sneaky thing and he produced a treat and he went 'Are you sure Conehead?' and having only eaten bread and water for such a long time I had to follow him. So anyway I jumped some jumps and sat on the box and did an awesome 'stand' and did some tunnels and I even did the big high dog-walk. Mummy had come prepared for any antics from the killer see-saw and had some specially steamed chicken ready so she gave some to Brian for his carry-out and then enticed me with the rest. Unfortunately the killer see-saw saw me coming and there was almost a major incident your honour and I fell off. I didn't run away though and stayed with the other big boys who were doing the fire-jumps so I played hide and seek with Brian with the small fire-jumps and we had so much fun that he nearly collapsed at the end. Anyway it was home-time then so he said we could all go as he was due back in the nursing home by 2:22 just before the match ended so he had to be quick. So I thought, I thought 'I know, I'll be quicker if I just take myself up the giant display team dog-walk and have a quick look at those Welsh mountains' and so I did it like a boss much to everyone's astonishment and then I jumped on the green box and did another fabulously perfect 'stand' and mummy looked like she was going to faint so I stopped there. I had a cuddle off my auntie Rita again at the end and she said I was dead boss and clever. I don't think this agility is quite as bad as I first thought your honour...

I did the big boys agility course again on Sunday with Sharon and even though I fell off the A frame I still did it again, I don't think I'm ever going to be happy with the killer see-saw though but I did go on it again with Sharon and I will keep trying. Sharon was really impressed with me because I went for a lie down without having to be told your honour I quite like having a lie down.

After the agility I went to meet the beautiful Flip she is only a few weeks old and as gorgeous as a border collie is allowed to be. Flip owns Kate and our Freya met her yesterday and said she was a flipping nuisance jumping at her all the time just like I used to. I like Flip, I just might be in Love. ❤

I will update you on my amazing adventures again just as soon as I can.

Love Timothy. xxxx

28th January 2017
Paul Newman's birthday.
Laddie is improving.

My name is Timothy and I'm a Border Collie and it has been four days since my last confession and our Laddie the Baddie can run again!

Oh it's been hectic here your honour with all this nursing again and everything and I'm just rushed off my feet and I've just got so much work to do and so I thought I would have a play with myself on the intersex while mummy has gone to work.

Laddie the Baddie is enjoying his fine dining experiences and just like Sir Lord Jack he has learned how to work mummy's head and if she dares offer Laddie anything other than fine dining he shakes his head and refuses it. Oh it's so much fun to watch and mummy is demented again keeping up with him and all the cooking she has to do for him. He is dining on smoked haddock this evening with seasonal vegetables and herbs.

To begin with Laddie was just so drunk and wobbly that he couldn't go for a walk but then he sobered up again but was only allowed a lead walk a little way up the lane and back. Today he came out with me and Freya for a bit of fun with our mates Ben and Ruby and he did really well and even managed to run, it was only about six or eight strides but he did do it.

We don't know how long he will be running with us though, Mr Dunn says we have to hope for the best and prepare for the worst and he is getting his medicine just one week at a time.

Mummy is demented and losing the plot and everything and yesterday she went into work commando style and her top of the range receptionist Jan told her off. I like Jan, she sends me sweeties because I am just so adorable and handsome.

Did you know I am learning how to walk? I am learning to walk

on two legs and I'm not too bad either, mummy says when I have
mastered it completely then she is going to send me into work to
do her job and she can play with herself on the intersex all day
long. I like learning new things and I showing Wendy and June
my new tricks too and then they give me some more to learn. It's
hard work being a handsome border collie.

I have to go now because it's time for Laddie's medicine and then I
have to go and water the herbs in the herb cellar.

I will write again as soon as I can.
Love Timothy. xxxx

Sunday 28th January 2017
Salmon en croute.

My name is Timothy Conehead the Invincible and I'm a border collie, it has been one week since my last confession and our Freya is in trouble.

Oh dear, I don't know where to start your honour so I'll just start with our Freya, well it was like this you see. She did a wee in the polygamy tunnel and you're not allowed to do wees there so she had to stand in detention and in disgrace with Sharon while mummy squirted something over her wee wee. Did you know that everybody laughs at Freya because she does everything so slowly and delicately but if you shouted 'bunnies' to her you would be shocked to see how fast she moves. I reckon she's after the sympathy vote.

So there I was thinking Brian was in the old peoples home having a rest and then I heard this rumour and it might not be right but I'll tell you anyway. I think Pauline who owns him has kidnapped him and eloped with him to Gretna Green so now you know but don't tell anyone will you. Anyway so anyway Pauline has caught a Scottish Unicorn and is going to bring it back to join our herd in Unicorn woods, oh it's all so very exciting.

So where was I then? Oh I know. Wendy and June have decided that I am just so dead clever like and handsome of course and it's mummy who is training me wrong and so they decided to knock mummy into shape in the polygamy tunnel, oh it was so funny and then Sharon joined in too! I don't know whether they are abducting mummy or adopting her but they are going to sort her out and anyway mummy has to do lots of homework so as she gets it right next time.

On Sunday we went to see mummy's friend in the puppy class. Louie who is a whippet and owns Joanne wasn't having one of his better days your honour and was being very naughty. Apparently he had been told off for disrupting the whole class and he was that naughty he had to be tied to a post. I don't think I've ever been quite that naughty ever, or not during torture training anyway.

Wendy, who had decided to stay in bed all day for a rest had sent June to keep an eye on mummy to make sure she was training me properly and just in case she needed knocking into shape again. I was really good at everything especially been sent for a lie down and stopping halfway home for a rest.

I was allowed to do the big boys agility again too. I say allowed but really I thought it was just far too cold to be bothering with all that nonsense and I went like this to June, I went 'Hey June can't you just let me go home now please as mummy has done really well today and we don't want to upset her by showing her the killer seesaw now do we?'
June went like this she went 'No!'

I was a bit shocked your honour and then sadly for me mummy asked Sue who is owned by Betty to join us in the ring of torture. We all ran round together but it was only me who had to jump jumps and run up the giant professional display team dog-walk just to see if I could spot mummy's friend Doris in North Wales. So anyway then I was once more faced with the killer seesaw only this one is not quite as bad as the one that originally attacked me and Sharon appeared like magic from a puff of smoke and so Sue, Sharon and mummy all enticed me with some quite interesting treats and although I almost fainted as the seesaw tipped very slowly I did in fact survive the experience once more. I got lots and lots and lots of praise and enticements so I think I might do it again next week.

Laddie the Baddie has decided that he is staying with us a bit longer as he quite likes all the extra attention he is getting and is becoming rather partial to his fine dining experiences. Today he is having Angus Aberdeen steak braised slowly with leeks and chartenay carrots. Tomorrows delight is to be salmon on croot and I've been told I have to cook it but I don't know what croot is and when I goggled it it didn't look good your honour no it didn't look good at all. Can someone send me the recipe please?

I have to go now I have so much work to do and I have to take our Laddie out for a walk next, I do hope I find some croot to sit the salmon on.

I will let you know how I get on.
Love Timothy. xxxx
P.S. I want to send Saphy and my mums friend Laney some love and special gentle hugs as Saphy had to go to The Bridge on Friday. I hope that they are all behaving themselves at Rainbow Bridge until it is time for us all to pass over to the land of light together.

I am enclosing exhibit A your honour, it is a picture of our Freya doing a peekaboo to show Sharon that she can be good and clever sometimes.

My name is Timothy Conehead the Invincible and I'm a border collie. It has been nearly two weeks since my last confession and there has been a complaint made to head office.

I've just been so busy this week that I haven't had time to update my diary and next thing I gets summoned to a meeting with the commandant [that's mummy in case you didn't guess] and so anyway there I am summoned to a special meeting just for me only to be told that my bread ration is to be reduced as there has been a complaint. Apparently my aunty Rita has told mummy that I need to get my paw out and move myself as she is unable to go to work unless she has read my update each Sunday and if she gets the sack then it's my fault and I will be for the high jump too!

I didn't know we had high jumps to learn, is this more terror training in store for me? That was a rectal question.

Well so you see it was like this I've been really splendid in last weeks community service your honour apart from being distracted temporarily when my mate Ben brought Wendy out to play with Ruby of course. Me and Ben have a nice crusty line going on with a little weed but don't tell anyone will you? That was a rectal question too just in case you didn't know.

So where was I then? Oh yes I know I was being remarkably obedient and handsome and I'm thinking that if I impress Sharon enough with my formidable skills she might just repel me for good behaviour your honour but there again she might just fall in love with me even more than she has done already and want me to stay forever. I'm not sure what to to for the best really.

Brian had been let out of the nursing home again and when I asked him about whether he had eloped last weekend he just went like this he went 'Listen here you Conehead don't be giving my Pauline any ideas with these daft stories you keep writing, she just went shopping for something. Okay?' I said nothing as I've found this is the safest way forward but then I thought, I thought 'I know I wonder if Pauline has bought a shotgun for the next time they elope?'

When Freya went to do her agility in her class on Saturday she was just coming to line up and Brian went like this he went "Come on old girl" Well our Freya was so shocked, she doesn't think Brian should be allowed to call mummy an old girl and neither do I, she still has all her teeth and hair and everything still works properly too.

I was rather good in my advanced lesson only moving out of position on just one occasion your honour and I even did the big boys agility course again and even though I hated it I did let Sharon help me over the display team killer seesaw. I'm not very partial to the noise these seesaws make but I'm not as bad as I used to be when I was first accosted.

Did you know that mummy is expecting a baby? No, neither did I but I'm sure she is. Well she's expecting something and I don't think it's one of those plain brown parcels that our postman who is probably still called Les but we haven't seen him for ages, yes that one. I'm not sure if he has left because he couldn't cope with mummy and all her special parcels or maybe he couldn't cope with being herded up the driveway and back down again every-time he delivered or maybe he has been in the herb cellar and has touched things that should never be touched.

I will let you know when I have more information.
Love Timothy. xxxx

My name is Timothy Conehead the Invincible and I'm a border collie. It has been four days since my last confession.

It seems to be becoming something of a habit your honour Sharon was missing again today and Brian had once more been dragged out of the nursing home. Freya heard somebody say something about pole dancing but we're not sure whether they meant pole vaulting so please don't quote me. I'm really not sure I could learn how to pole vault your honour but I do have a sexy little swagger so I could learn how to dance.

Freya tells me that she continues to improve and wonders whether she will get a certificate for her CV when her community service ends.

My advanced class wasn't very advanced this week as somebody forgot to tell anyone it was on. We had Su who is owned by the beautiful Betty and Flo who had brought her mum up from London for the weekend, she had never been to a class before but did really well to be fair and Ann was handled by Troy I had a tiny problem with those menacing cones again and was once more excellent at being sent away for a lie down.

Su aided and abetted my trip around the display team torture course, I like Su and I quite liked her manky cheese and so I even did the killer seesaw twice but with my eyes closed at the OMG moment in the middle. I have once more survived this ordeal and will live to tell many more tales.
Sharon came in at the end and she was very pretty in her work clothes but I couldn't tell whether they were pole dancing clothes or not your honour.

Laddie the Baddie is still doing really well and is only slightly tipsy now, I keep him away from the wine cellar as much as I can but it's not easy. His fine dining delights continue but I never did find the croot to serve his salmon on. Tonight he is having braised steak with seasonal vegetables but I'm a bit stuck for tomorrow as I am supposed to be cooking him fishy suarez but I can't find the recipe anywhere, can any of yoos lot help me out here please?

I had a jolly good time on the Sunday with Sharon and was told I might be getting a bronze medal soon but only if I can do heel work without a treat in mummy's hand. Hmmm I'm excellent at doing things for bribes but I'm not sure I'm prepared to work for no treat. Isn't that against the law.

On the way out Sharon was talking to mummy again about expecting a baby, I'm not sure when she is expecting it though.

I will let you know as soon as I have more information.
Love Timothy. xxxx

P.S. I am attaching a picture of the valentines card I received this morning your honour, it seems Shayla is in love with me and to be fair who can blame her for falling for such a handsome legend as myself. I'm not sure that mummy would approve though as she is a bit doggist, I'm not sure if that's the same as being racist but I'm only supposed to have girlfriends who are border collies because we are the master race – I think that's what she said but I might be wrong.

A Visitation.

My name is Timothy Conehead the Invincible and I'm a border collie. It has been two days since my last confession and has anyone lost a pretty furry thing?

Hello everyone and thank you for all your good wishes for St Valentines day, I was knee deep in cards as you would expect from one so handsome and gorgeous and a legend in their own mind.

I wanted to let you know that our Laddie is getting fitter and fitter and decided he is staying around for a while longer as he especially likes the chocolate treats that Wendy brings for him on our walks. I never get any of course all the specialty feeding is reserved for old codgers it seems.

Anyway so anyway something strange happened today and I'm not sure what to think of it so maybe you can help me.

We had a visit today you see from Alex at Dogs Trust Merseyside and she brought this little tiny furry thing with her to play with us, I don't really know why she brought her your honour because we have great fun playing with ourselves here everyday without needing extra help and things.

She is really very pretty but her mummy who works on a farm was getting fed up with her and was attacking her so she left home and went to live with Alex for a while. Apparently we are going to visit her again on Monday but I don't know why, perhaps it's part of my community service but I'm not sure.

I will keep you posted if I hear anything else.
Love Timothy. xxxx

P.S. I am enclosing exhibit A which is a picture of this tiny furry thing trying to attack our Laddie while she was inspecting her new pack.

Sunday 18th February 2017
Shayla's 2nd birthday.

My name is Timothy and I'm a border collie, it has been three days since my last confession and who is this Jennifer?

I'm getting more confused here your honour by the day. Some strange things are happening and I've heard mummy talking to her imaginary friend again on the phone, does anyone know who Jennifer is please?

I think mummy has picked up someone else's shopping by mistake, something isn't right. You see it's like this, there I was putting the shopping away as usual only I've noticed that there is some puppy food in there and we haven't got any puppies oh look there are puppy pads too is that like an Ipad but for a puppy?

You see what it is, is well we were going to foster Pollyanna who doesn't like being in the rescue centre and so the lady was coming to see mummy about it but she couldn't because she was busy with some puppies and now Pollyanna isn't coming to stay for a while anymore but I don't know why.

Anyway in community service we did lots of work and apparently I might be getting a bronze medal soon for being so unbelievably handsome and cool, apparently I'm not bad at all at most things and I could one day get a gold medal for lying down for a nap while mummy goes into the polygamy tunnel fir a quick shot of something and not moving an inch while she was gone.

I did the skyscraper dog walk all on my own like a boss! I did need Sharon to help me over the seesaw though but I did do it, on our way out Lynn said the Jennifer was going to put me to shame. Who is this Jennifer...?

We did more medal training on Sunday and Sharon said I was gold medal standard for stopping in an emergency but needed emergency work with following mummy without a treat. Wendy kept telling mummy off for dropping treats and said mummy was an old bag, oh no – it wasn't that she said mummy should get an old bag to put the treats in instead of her pocket. I think.

It was Shayla's birthday today and June let us kiss lots of times at school but we didn't get to have fun behind the bike sheds, maybe tomorrow.

I will write again when I know more.
Love Timothy xxxx

HAPPY 2ND BIRTHDAY
Love from
Timothy xxxx

Monday 20th February 2017
Jennifer Eccles-Phythian Day.

My name is Timothy Conehead the Invincible and I'm a border collie. It has been just one day since mt last confession and I have bad news, very bad news indeed.

It was like this you see, we were informed by the commander that we were going on a very special message so you see I thought like this I thought 'I know we'll be going to buy Laddie the Baddie some fine dining experiences that I will have to cook and so I can smell all the wonderful smells and dream about them while I eat my piece of bread later' and so I smiled sweetly as only I can and got into the chariot.

We seemed to be driving a long time and so I thought like this I thought 'We must be going to a very special shop that is just a long way away.' When we stopped though it wasn't a shop and lots of dogs being walked by the volunteer walkers and then mummy disappeared. When she came out she was holding that pretty furry thing that came to play with us last week.

So you see this fluffy ball is called Jennifer and mummy say's it is my job to make sure she is good and perfect in every way and not naughty ever, she mustn't know it's another border collie your honour. Laddie the Baddie is allowed to kiss her but not allowed to teach her anything bad otherwise he is to be sent for training to do the high jump! I don't know where we keep the high jump at torture training though, I'll have to ask Sharon or Brian the next time that I go.

I am not allowed to tell Jennifer about the killer seesaw from Nemesis or the dodgy dog-walk or the cunning cones. I suppose I'll have to teach her to cook and everything, our Freya say's she's not borrowing any of her clothes or make-up especially her Christmas party frock and bow.

Oh it's just awful and I don't know how I'm going to cope, Jennifer keeps trying to get my tail and she wants a lift on Laddies back and he's not a bit happy. He won't let her get on his couch or anything. Freya's not too happy either as Jennifer keeps wanting to latch on for a feed. And she really wasn't happy at all when Jennifer attached herself to Freya's tail and didn't let go when mummy called Freya to her. I think she might want to be in a circus!

 Wendy who came to check we were all looking after her properly was no help at all as she just kept laughing. Oh it's just dreadful your honour, we are hoping that Alex comes back for her soon but think she might be staying for a while.

We think she looks more like postman Pat's cat than a border collie, I wonder if she is any good at hunting..
I will tell you more if I survive the night.

Love Timothy. xxxx

Tuesday 21st February 2017
Time for Bed said Zebedee.

My name is Timothy Conehead the Invincible and I'm a border collie. It has been one day since my last confession and I'm not best pleased.

So you see we all missed being The Fab Four after Sir Lord Jack had to go but we were all reasonably happy at being The Three Musketeers and having to do community service at the torture training camp and then this little furry thing called Jennifer came along.
Anyway so after terrifying most of the life out of us for hours it was eventually time to go to bed with Zebedee again.

All went well. When I say all went well what I really mean is that once Jennifer had stopped crying for mummy when we went to bed at ten she slept like a baby until half past one. I suppose that is because she is a baby I imagine. So when she woke us up at 1:30 am we were not amused, we were not very amused at all your honour and our Freya went like this she went 'Listen you Jennifer I know you are really a cat in a border collie suit and mummy will suss it soon and if you don't be quiet and go to sleep I will flatten you tomorrow, literally. Okay? It was a rectal question and I'm not sure if Jennifer knew but she went back to sleep quick. I was having a lovely dream about Shayla who is going to be in charge of my harem and everything if June lets me have one and it was a lovely dream and then at 5:30 a cat came to look through the window and our Laddie wasn't a bit happy so he shouted at the cat to go away We think that he might have just woke mummy up and it definitely woke Jennifer up and she had another cry but then she went back to sleep.
Anyway so anyway mummy got up earlier than usual and cooked us breakfast and Jennifer tried to eat Laddies dinner and Laddie wasn't a bit flocking happy your honour, he wasn't very flocking happy at all. Jennifer had to be dessicated in the dining room so as we could eat our breakfast in peace. Mummy took Freya upstairs with her for safe keeping then just in case Jennifer attacked her or

anything while she got ready. She left me and Laddie to babysit so I hid in the dining room while Jennifer kept Laddie prisoner on his own sofa.

It's just awful your honour, she just cries or attacks us and we don't know what to do with her. Mummy says it is like having a ball and chain on your leg only it's a Jennifer that has come for a free ride. I'll let you know if the fairies come and take her in the night.

Love Timothy. xxxx

Wednesday 22nd February 2017.
The birth is officially registered.

.My name is Timothy Conehead the Invincible and I'm a border collie. It has been one day since my last confession and has anyone got any paracetamol to spare please?

So where was I? Oh I know we were trying to ignore this cat in a border collie suit only it won't let us ignore it at all. So anyway this Jennifer seems to think it is okay to open mummy's mail when she isn't looking and rip it up and stuff and she has had mummy's appointments diary out and erm she may have damaged a twenty pound note your honour. We are hoping this is punishable with a long term prison sentence we just need to know who to report it to.

Well anyway breakfast began with exclusion for Jennifer as she stole a big piece of chicken skin off Laddies dish and it's just got to stop. She doesn't seem very interested in her own food but wants to eat ours.

When it was time for our walkies we snook out without her and went to meet our mates and we are not too happy because we don't seem to be getting quite as long as usual because mummy likes to get back to check on the baby. The baby?

Anyway we went on a message to get Laddies medicine and to register Jennifer with the vet. Consultations had ended so there was only the staff there and oh if you'd have seen them all fussing about over this naughty little girl. Three vets were on duty and all three of them had to come out to see the adorable little puppy along with the vets nurses and reception staff, it's a vets for goodness sake you'd think they saw enough puppies without needing to drool over the naughty one. They all think it's funny as they know it's mummy's first puppy. Lisa wanted to know what her full name was so mummy told them it was Jennifer Eccles Phythian [The Boss] and everyone approved, she has now duly been registered.

When we got home mummy decided she just needed forty winks and we're not sure whether she has been bugged or deprived of a bit if sleep, so she had a lie down. It was really, really quiet so I thought 'I know, me and Freya could have some fun with these plastic bottles that we've got that are really noisy when you chew them and throw them around' and so we did . Mummy opened her eyes and looked at us, she didn't say anything but she didn't look really happy to be fair so me and Freya thought 'I know we'll see if we can have some fun and make mummy happy' and so we jumped on her on the couch and oh we had so much fun that mummy was nearly crying laughing, well we're not sure about the laughing bit.

I think we might be having an early night as mummy is looking just a bit tired and doesn't want Wendy and June laughing at her again tomorrow.

I will update you when I can..
Love Timothy. xxxx

My name is Timothy Conehead the Invincible and I'm a border collie. It has been just one day since my last confession.

Oh it just gets worse your honour we fear for our lives with Storm Jennifer. The book I bought said it would get better each day but it isn't, it just isn't. She just cries and cries and mummy refuses to do on demand feeding she says Jennifer's teeth are far too sharp to be going down that route.

We had a great plan to escape and we left a note out during our morning walk offering a reward for anyone who could come and rescue us. I very cleverly attached my name tag so people would know where to come to rescue us from. So anyway we were all excited and patiently waiting and wondering who it was who would come for us oh and we insisted on no puppies either. We tried not to look too excited or anything and even pretended we didn't mind Jennifer lunging at us and then all our dreams were squished when Wendy turned up with my name tag! She said she found it but didn't say anything about the note, we are hoping she doesn't tell mummy.

We think Jennifer might be planning on writing a book one day as she seems really keen on stealing mummy's pens, the good thing is mummy is getting tidier and seems to be practicing her new language skills more.

After Jennifer finally passed out from all the harassment she had been inflicting on us we ventured out but discovered storm Doris was worse than storm Jennifer so we didn't stay too long.

Storm Jennifer settled down for a while in exile while mummy escaped to work and then proceeded to annihilate us when mummy returned.

We are now preparing for bed and hope storm Jennifer doesn't cry for too long.

I will update you as soon as I can.
Love Timothy xxxx

Is anyone looking to adopt some refugees?

My name is Timothy and I'm a border collie and it has only been
one day since my last confession and I need your help please.

Oh I don't know where to start. Is anybody looking for three
refugees called Laddie the Baddie, Freya the Hunter and Timothy
Conehead the Invincible please? We feel we have no option but to
flee our homeland at Love House as it has been desiccated by
storm Jennifer and we can no longer cope. We have tried building
a wall but she Trumps that much she takes off and flies over it!

Mummy said that if I read Jennifer a nice story at bedtime that she
might not cry so I read her a ghost story and she cried even more.
How was I to know she would be scared of ghosts? She did sleep
right through though after her initial crying for mummy so maybe
the ghost story did work.

Laddie is just getting fed up with her hitching a ride every time he
walks past her and me and our Freya are running out of our white
tips on our tails because she keeps grabbing them and hoping for a
a quick thrill up the drive, if I run out of white hair on my tail I
might be defrocked from border collie status and then where will I
be?
I'm looking forward to torture training at the weekend when
hopefully I will get a break from her, I wonder if I could sell her
to anyone without mummy noticing..

I will let you know how I get one.
Love Timothy xxxx

My name is Timothy Conehead the Invincible and I'm a border collie. It has been three days since my last confession.

All was quiet on the West Lancs front. Well when I say all was quiet what I really mean is that I'd managed to escape storm Jennifer to continue with my community service only because she has disturbed my beauty sleep all week I can't remember what happened now. I remember that everyone was asking how she was but that no one was asking how me and our Freya or Laddie were coping but we managed to get through our training without incident.

I wasn't very happy on the Sunday your honour to discover she had been loaded into the chariot and was coming to torture training with me. I was pretty marvellous it has to be said apart from being spooked by the killer see-saw that was playing with itself in the wind. Mummy forgot to bring me a toy and I was forced to play with a dead rabbit that Brian had in his pocket, he must have really manky pockets.

When it came to time for the torture course Sharon could see I was in need of a valium so she decided to send me to the big boys course to do the see-saw there and although I was still scared I did it without jumping off and without needing to be held, I think it is Sharon's treats that I like and I might do it again because I got lots of praise and treats and hugs.

Afterwards I was imprisoned in the chariot while everyone came to meet the baby oh it was awful, she isn't nearly as handsome as me, I was expecting champagne to appear any minute as everyone cooed over the little whinger.

The infant is sleeping soundly as I write my blog cuddled up next to our Freya and lying on top of Scampi the border collie doorstop, long may this peace continue.

I will write again as soon as I can.
Love Timothy. xxxx

My name is Timothy Conehead the Invincible and I'm a border collie. It has been one day since my last confession and I need help with the wild child.

You see it's like this your honour, I know when I came to be corrected in Kathleen's house of correction I had no manners. I also admit I had to do a sit stay in the next room while Sir Lord Jack, Laddie the Baddie and Freya the Hunter were fed but I wasn't this wild your honour, no one could be this wild.

The wild child has good recall sometimes and has also learned how to sit and knows this action gets a reward too so often comes to mummy and sits in front of her expectantly, mummy say's she is going to be a nightmare. I'm a bit confused about the 'going to be' part of that statement. She refuses to learn what stay is as yet. I saw mummy writing hammer and nails on her shopping list, I'm not sure what these are for though.

Anyway so anyway we have a pecking order still only when Laddie gets fed Jennifer becomes supersonic and gets into his dish before him. So storm Jennifer wild child extraordinaire has to be airlifted into mummy's arms where she wriggles but from this position Laddie can safely be fed and then Freya and then gorgeous handsome me. When mummy has completed this task she then collects Jennifer's bowl and ejects the wild child back to ground level for feeding. We have posh non-slip bowls to keep us chained in one space but Jennifer has a metal dish and she zooms around the kitchen tiles with her bowl and it is quite scary to see how fast she moves and every so often she zooms away from her bowl into Laddies and has to be emergency airlifted away. Oh it's a nightmare.
I will keep you updated on my suffering as soon as I can.
Love Timothy. xxxx

Wednesday 8th March 2017
The Storm Brews.
Jennifer has a family reunion..

My name is Timothy Conehead the Invincible and I'm a border collie. has been eight days since my last confession and life continues It to be hectic here,

Oh where to start? It is just a nightmare and if it doesn't stop we'll need to rename our house your honour.

Well you see so apparently there have been complaints about my irregular motions concerning my blog. Can you believe that? So anyway I've been down to the cellar and sobered the judge up with a little something I have growing in the illegal herb cellar. I had a word in his shell like and then consulted my legal team who all tell me without prejudice your honour that I can flocking well post whenever I want to.

I still would just like to say that I'm dreadfully sorry your honour for not writing for such a long time but you see mummy has been sick with gastronomical enteritis and galloping hob knobs and with the noises she has been making I think she may have had malaria and leprosy as well. She has been chained between the toilet and the laptop and it has not been poetry in motion I can tell you. So in between my work and my community service I have been reading a very very old medical dictionary I found while I've been locked in the cellar on herb duty. I think she might have had the pox too but I'm not sure.

So where were we, well it's like this you see, this wild child appears to be a permanent feature here now, I have tried to repel it but I couldn't find no veils.

The child prodigy can do a sit and she can also do a fifteen second sit stay, I don't know what all the fuss is about I can do two minutes with mummy hiding in the polygamy tunnel. Oh I nearly forgot she is also pretty good on recall and is learning that NO!!!

means you are not allowed to jump all over our Laddie and bite him while you're there. She does it to me and Freya but we chase her better than Laddie can.

It seems she gets loaded into our chariot most times we go on a message now. She was even with us when we went for our community service which passed without incident and I once more managed to cross the killer see-saw with Sharon's help. At the end my aunty Rita was there and we had lovely proper cuddles just because we could. There was a boy there called Cornelius and I think he belonged to her, well anyway he was cuddling the wild child and was wanting to know if he could take her home and I was working so hard at teleporting my aunty Rita to say yes with my mind but she didn't, I think she may have been already engaged or needed to be charged up a bit more but I'm not sure. Aunty Rita said that Jennifer had to go home with Timothy, I wonder if it is a punishment.

Mummy said that if you got gold medals for looking drop dead gorgeous in an identity parade then I would need another cellar just for my medals. I continue to impress everyone with my emergency stop and the emergency work on my being able to follow mummy without a treat to bribe me seems to be working too, she kidded me she had a treat in her hand and she didn't but I followed her anyway just in case. It was ok though as I was given a bribe right at the end.

I was so excited on Monday as mummy said we were going on another special journey like we did a couple of weeks ago. It was a long journey again and I thought, I thought 'I know, I'll bet we have had the wild child on one of those sale or return things or maybe on a two week trial and we are taking her back' Oh I was so excited and I was right because we arrived at Dogs Trust Huyton. I noticed that Wendy had come with us and I thought 'I know, I'll bet June told Wendy to make mummy take her back due to her beating us all up. So Wendy and mummy got out of the chariot and took the wild child out and disappeared. Oh I was so excited I thought I was going to burst but apparently they had all gone for a family reunion and to have their second jabs.

After a while mummy burst my bubble and arrived back with the wild child under her arm. I heard her talking to Wendy about training and apparently in two weeks time Storm Jennifer will be going to torture training too, she'll have to do more than a fifteen second sit stay if she wants to win any medals though.

I'm just going back to the cellar for another read of my medical dictionary, the bubonic plague looks interesting and I'm thinking she might have had the black fever too.

I will write more as soon as I can.

Love Timothy. xxxx

Friday 10th March 2017
Jennifer is a water baby.

My name is Timothy Conehead the Invincible and I'm a border collie. It has been two days since my last confession and mummy is nearly better.

So you see earlier in the week when mummy was really poorly with the bubonic plaque and the black death she was feeling really dizzy and hot and she was hallucinating but we don't think it was the drugs your honour. So she said she would have to have a lie down. So she did say to us she said 'Now be good or else!' So you see we thought 'I know if we just all cuddle mummy it might make her feel better' Our Laddie said to me 'Push off Conehead I'm staying on my couch and spying out of the window for the postman in case he has any dodgy plain brown paper parcels' and so we left him there.

Me and Freya waited for mummy to settle down on the other couch and then Freya climbed on her head end and cuddled her and I climbed on her feet end and cuddled her and then guess what? Well you see Jennifer wild child Eccles decided to come and cuddle the mummy too just so she would feel better. Jennifer thought it was best to have a drink first but what most of you don't know is that when Jennifer has a drink she puts her two front feet in the bowl first to stir it up, so she did this you see and then she did climb on the mummy and she climbed all the way up and cuddled mummy in the middle with her wet feet.

Mummy must of liked it as she kept saying 'great, this is just great' and 'Oh flock, what did I do to deserve this' and 'Oh fantastic, just what I wanted' 'perfect just perfect, just what I was hoping for.' and she was crying laughing again. I think she was laughing anyway.

We really like making mummy happy.

Love Timothy xxxx

P.S. I am enclosing exhibit A your honour Jennifer stirring the water.

My name is Timothy Conehead the Invincible and I'm a border collie it was been three days since my last confession.

So where were we, oh I know. There was a lap dancing competition in Formby on Saturday and Sharon was awol again, I"m not sure if there is a connection. Sergeant Major Brian was in charge of torture training on Saturday your honour and oh it was just terrible. Our Freya said he was picking on mummy because she kept asking too many questions and should know better and was told to 'walk or else' so mummy had to walk past the identity parade line and they all hissed and booed as she passed, Freya didn't know what to do. A little later mummy got told off for playing with her balls in class and then Wendy made mummy show everyone her balls, in front of the whole class! Freya said it was so embarrassing and they were all laughing at her too.

The wild child has now signed up for puppy classes to begin next Saturday and she has put her name down to do the bronze medal in April.

I don't remember anyone cooing over me when I started going training but it's all 'Oh lets see Jennifer,' How is the baby' 'Is she being good for you?' and me and our Freya have to just sit there and listen to it all. They have no idea of what we have to put up with your honour.

Anyway so anyway I'm getting much better at the agility and Brian who was out on day release but we don't know whether he was tagged or not, well he showed mummy how to do the weave with me properly and now I'm just dead boss we missed the seesaw out because Brian doesn't use the same treats as Sharon so I just thought 'I know, I'll just wait until Sharon wants me to do the seesaw and I'll do it then' so I did. We're not really sure what Brian has been up to but he is on rations now, we think he might be going commando next week and he'll need his ration book then but we're not sure.

So you see we did bronze medal training on both torture training days again and I passed twice again but I have to pass it again next Sunday if I want a proper medal. I got accused of interfering with Pauline and Dipstick and Brian said 'Just watch it you Conehead or else' but Pauline said it wasn't my fault and she just slipped so it was ok. Our Freya is on the emergency list for a cancellation for the second bronze medal class next Sunday and she reckons she is better than me at bronze she can't do a gold standard emergency stop though like I can!

We don't know what happened to Wendy, we think she forgot to get up or she forgot it was Sunday or she forgot to go to training until it was nearly all over and then she remembered just in time for team training. I'll see if she would like to borrow storm Jennifer as an alarm clock.

I got a special commendation from June for being such a gentleman and getting Shayla's kong and bringing it to her and then June helped me with the seesaw and I got lots of treats especially as I did the weaves again dead quick.

Sharon knows that the killer seesaw gives me a nervous breakdown so she sent me straight to the big boys torture training and said I had to jump all the jumps on number two height, so I did. When Sharon say's jump well you just jolly well jump.

Feeding time continues to be an experience here your honour and while the mummy is adding the dried food to our dinners the wild child likes to get into the food cupboard to explore, once she has been evicted from the cupboard then she knows it is feeding time and puts her arms up for mummy to airlift her up so she can watch from a safe distance as we all get fed first and can't eat our dinners by mistake.
I will write again soon,
Love Timothy xxxx

Wednesday 15th March 2017
Journey Into the unknown.

My name is Timothy Conehead the Invincible and I'm a border collie. It has been three days since my last confession.

Twinkle twinkle little start, how I wonder what you are. Mummy said I was a star but now it seems that storm Jennifer is glowing more brightly.

She jumps into mummy's arms now whenever she wants to but I'm not allowed to, oh no it's "Timothy have you watered the herbs in the herb cellar and replaced any missing bulbs down there, have you cleaned out the moat and is the judge still in the wine cellar?" All the time Jennifer Eccles is getting extra cuddles from the mummy.

She is allowed out with us big boys now but she has to be on a three metre line just in case she forgets who she is with, as if. I'm pretty dam sure she knows she is Jennifer Eccles & The Boss of our pack. She tries to keep up with us too but mummy can't run as fast as we can, she followed me and our Freya into the undergrowth and wasn't a bit scared either. I am keeping my paws crossed for our Freya to get the wanderlust in a few weeks and go off on an adventure with the wild child and erm perhaps mislay her.

Every time we go out on a message she gets to sit in the back of our chariot with us to see if she is big enough yet, Laddie is pleased to say that she is not and we are all hoping that she remains a prisoner in her cage for a very long time your honour, a very long time indeed.

I don't think we are allowed to see June and Wendy anymore for a while, I think it's in case the wild child attacks their fur babies or it could be that they are practicing for the Olympics but I'm not sure. I miss my girlfriend Shayla too.

Laddie had Angus Aberdeen mince with chantenay carrots for dinner this evening and I know the wild child had some too, us poorly fed dogs had our usual ration of bread and we've got no more special treats left that mummy's top of the range receptionist Jan sent me. Life is just so hard.

If I survive the night I will write again soon. xxxx

I am enclosing exhibit A your honour, me and my special friend Jan went I went to see her at mummy's work.

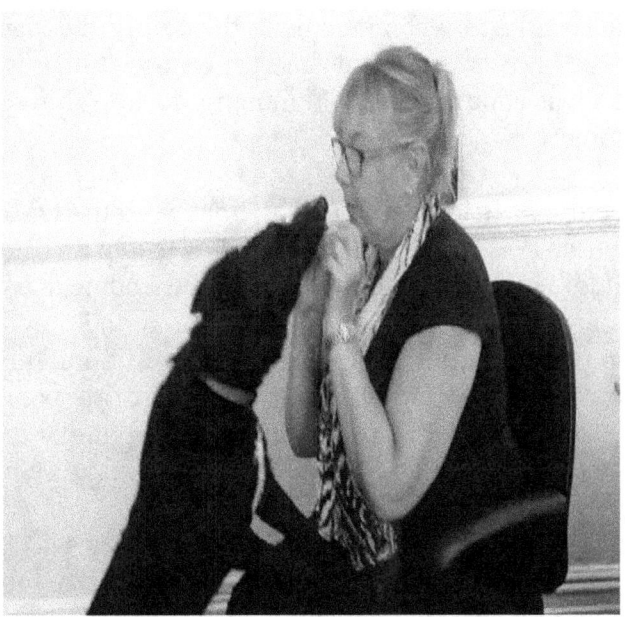

Saturday 18th March 2017
Jennifer's first day at school.

My name is Timothy Conehead the Invincible and I'm a border collie and it has been three days since my last confession.

Saturday was Jennifer Eccles Phythian's first day at school and as all kids do she had her photograph taken before she went. Jennifer came from Anglesey and had to be fostered from five weeks old so her foster mum Janene and her foster dad came to see her perform at her first day at school.
Apparently she was ok at following mummy with a treat and excellent at recall and when it came to the agility she wasn't phased by the killer seesaw and aced the dog-walk like well, like a Boss! Brian was shocked and told mummy to stop showing off with her homework.

We found out that Brian, you know the one with the tag who is out on day release – yes that one - well he has just had vestibula just like our Laddie so we're thinking that maybe Laddie sneaked him into the wine cellar when mummy was at work and they have been playing gin rummy with the judge down there. I think gin rummy is when you have a shot of gin and then a shot of rum and then you get blindfolded and have a go at pinning the tail on the camel. if you survive to get to do it all over again. I think that's what it is.

I was so excited to see Sharon on Saturday and she said I could go home and live with her and she would feed me lovely food and everything and I was so excited and then she said that if I accepted that I would have to do community service and the torture course on three extra days a week, I nearly fainted. I think I will remain enslaved at Love House for a while longer then.

My aunty Rita wasn't there to give me cuddles either and I failed my next to last rehearsal for the bronze medal because when they were doing the mingling and chatting bit I decided to join in and I wasn't supposed to. It was ok though because I found out that that was the rehearsal for the silver medal the following week.

Mummy was so tired because she did three hours at torture training and then when we got home we all had to go for a walk so as our Laddie doesn't seize up or anything. And so we did and then mummy had to do some writing on the intersex and she was busy writing away and then she thought "I know, when I just finish these last five hundred words I'll just have a quick nap" only when she looked to see where she might have this nap she noticed that there wasn't any room on any of the couches because we all needed a nap too. So the mummy just thought "I know I'll just keep working and hope my eyes stay open " and so she did.

Then Wendy called in because she couldn't remember her way home and thought we might know but I don't think she is going to call in again as she got mugged by all of us and I'm not sure she can take it. Mummy trained me how to smile you see only I'm not sure she thought it through properly as when I smile I show you all of my teeth. and I'm trying to hug you at the same time. I think I look awesome.

So anyway mummy went to bed and was disturbed by Laddie in the night who just needed a glass of water and a hug and another bedtime story so she wasn't best pleased at all because she was doing five classes on the Sunday. I say five classes but it was only three and then two exams just thrown in for fun.

In the puppy class Jennifer showed off all mummy's homework again, she can do a sit a stand and a down now and her recall is A*+ and she whizzed her way through agility and then said what next?

Our Freya did her last dress rehearsal for her bronze medal and I was allowed to join in with the team training. Sharon has said that I'm improving so much that I can join in with the team training every week now and it was great fun we played hide and seek with the hula hoops and I managed a jump with Shayla but I couldn't do it with Luna as I was just so worn out.

Mummy was shattered after our three classes and just wanted to go home but she couldn't because we had to be tested to see if we had learned enough to be awarded a bronze certificate, so she stayed.

Wendy and June kept making fun of her because she was so tired so she went like this she went 'If you don't stop picking on me I will get my Timothy to smile at you and that'll soon shut you up' They didn't take any notice of her though, they never do to be honest.

So where were we then, oh yes I know. I was just superb at being handsome and I didn't join in any conversations with anyone who might not have invited me to. Shayla was excellent too and Luna was on her best behaviour for Ethan but Rubyroo moaned and chunnered the whole way through our exam. It didn't matter though because we all passed and got a bronze certificate and a photograph and everyone was really pleased, except for mummy because she had to do it all again with our Freya.

Our Freya is lovely and also a nark so mummy had to give her lots of herbs from the herb cellar and we were pleased to hear that there was no compulsory pee test to pass. Angela who is owned by many but had Lily pop in charge of her that day kept mummy awake mostly by laughing at her. Freya behaved herself in a groovy sort of way and she only nearly reacted once so mummy gave her one of her looks and she settled down again.

I do think mummy was a little overtired though she was asked the same question twice about one of the rules the country-code for me she said collecting poo for souvenirs and taking it home and then for Freya she said it was to take your litter home and then she remembered it was a dog test so she threw poo in quickly. She does need to do some reading up though because when she was asked what sort of buildings would you not expect to take your dog into and mummy said 'a church' I really think she was sleepwalking at this point and hoping for divine intervention and when our lovely examiner Andrea laughed she quickly said and shops and restaurants. Surprisingly our Freya also passed and she got a bronze certificate and a photograph too.

Then it was time for mummy to go home and she had to take us all for walkies too and I think by this time she didn't know what her name was because she was so tired but we helped her and kept her cuddled on the couch, we let her have a bit of it until it was time to go to bed with Zebedee..

The good news is I am now entered for the silver medal to be tested next Sunday and mummy reckons the wild child is going to be entered for the bronze medal in a few weeks time in April. Mummy says that if she can get enough homework done and get her to do a minute 'stay' then she could pass, she can already do a 30 second stay. We are thinking we will lace her dinner with a few specially selected herbs, it's either that or hammer and nails but we think the others might notice the blood.

I will write again soon.
Love Timothy xxxx
Certified Bronze Medalist 2017.

March 23rd 2017
Jennifer the Cat.

My name is Timothy Conehead the Invincible and I'm a border collie. It was been four days since my last confession and I'm sure Jennifer is a cat.

Oh it's just awful here your honour and it just gets worse. You see it's like this mummy said she almost lost her mind many years ago when she had two kittens because they were just so wild and it seems that I was right and that Storm Jennifer is really a cat in a border collie suit. I don't think mummy is very happy because she climbs the curtains and everything.

She climbs the welsh dresser to play with mummy's special ornaments, she climbs on the window sills to chat to the unicorns and pegasus and she even found a way to climb onto the breakfast bar in the dining room and now that part has been sealed off until crime watch come to investigate. We now have to live in solitary confinement in the other half of the room while Laddie gets to lounge around on the sofas in the lounge.

When mummy just walks along and she is in a day dream and Jennifer just throws herself at her and grabs her leg or her trousers and mummy cries like this she goes "Oh for flocks sake Jennifer I am not your plaything!"

We had this really nice paper basket as well you see, I say paper basket but really it was made of straw or raphael or something and anyway it was a top of the range paper basket and it had a lining and everything and now we haven't got one anymore. I think we have a metal paper basket on our shopping list now and we have to take our rubbish all the way out to the other bins until we get one . I'm struggling to understand how a paper basket can be metal though.

I was really good when I first came here because all I used to do was to empty all the contents of the paper basket out all over the floor and make nice patterns for mummy but storm Jennifer has destroyed our top of the range basket completely. I'll bet she gets community service too and rightly so your honour,

Life is just so hectic here.

I will keep you updated when I can.

Love Timothy xxxx
Certified Bronze medalist 2017

My name is Timothy Conehead the Invincible and I'm a border collie, it has been two days since my last confession.

Oh there has just been so much happening here and I'm not sure where to start your honour.

Do you remember that I was awarded the bronze certificate last week for being outstandingly handsome amongst other things? Well this week we decided to see if I could do the double and get the silver too, so mummy has been working hard with me in between running around like a headless chicken with our Jennifer who has entered for the bronze certificate in six weeks time and work. The wild child is still in nappies for goodness sake but she does have one mean recall and can do sit, stand and down and almost do a finish too so who knows.

Anyway where was I then? Oh yes so mummy remembered to turn up to all three classes on Saturday and she wasn't quite as bad as last week, we keep giving her a shot of philisan and some special herbs and she is getting much better, I think. Jennifer once more charmed and amazed everyone with her skills while Freya continued to be a nark but she wasn't too bad really and providing she can do the mingling without giving anyone a black eye she could easily pass the silver too.

Moving on to gorgeous me well, what can I say? We did a dress rehearsal for the silver medal and Sharon couldn't open the gate because it had this big chain thing on it that looked like a chastity belt so she knew Brian would know how to open it and she sent him to look for a key and you could just tell he was used to undoing such things and so he did it. So anyway, we went for a walk on the motorway and we had to ignore a strange lady pushing a pram that had frankly seen better days your honour and a bike which had no chain. I think Wendy did something to distract us too, it could have been a strip or anything but I was so good I didn't even look. Then we had to show that we knew how to sit and look both ways to cross the road so Sharon was the lollipop lady and we all crossed but I didn't see any green men. We had to ignore Brian too but it was difficult to ignore the stunning red setter he had with him.

When we got back to school I passed the not jumping up part because mummy was holding me down with her foot but when we got to the part were we have to be examined by someone else I just got so excited and wanted a cuddle, so I failed. Mummy then spent the next half hour taking me around everyone so they could examine me and eventually I understood.

When I say mummy is getting used to doing three classes in a row one day after another I may have exaggerated just a bit and she wasn't very happy at all your honour to be losing an hour as well as having another exam at the end but we have her trained well and we got her all ready to go in again on the Sunday.

We had been a given special request from Sharon appealing for some bespoke herbs to be brought in to speed some of the dogs up and slow some of them down so we brought them with us but not before mummy managed to slip me a mickey finn so as I wouldn't panic if the killer see-saw looked at me or anything. So anyway, Jennifer did her class and mummy was laughing about the way our Jennifer sits and Sharon said it really wasn't very ladylike and as mummy was taking her turn to file past the identity parade Sharon said 'mind you they do say that dogs take after their owners don't they?' Mummy was crying laughing again, I think she was laughing, I mean it's not like the booze liners are due in yet to supplement our income or anything is it?

It was our Freya's turn to shine next and no one wanted to stand next to her except Ruby who is her best mate. We think Freya is going through a mid life crisis and may need stronger herbs than the ones she has been getting but mostly she was good.

Then it was time for our final dress rehearsal for the silver awards and Brian was there with the chastity belt key again and he said that as I was looking so amazingly handsome this week and that I should lead the rabble out. So off we went to play on the motorway again being careful to ignore the bike with no chain and the pram with no baby and Brian who had a different dog but I didn't look at it honestly. After that we had fun with Sharon playing X marks the spot and Y are we all still here oh and Peek-a-boo. Everyone kept telling Wendy off though for singing 'Shall we dance; from The King and I' and mummy got the blame because she started it and if she does it again she will be in big trouble.

Then it was time for the testing.

To begin with Andrea who is our lovely examiner checked that we all knew our names and things and where we lived and stuff oh and we had to show everyone that we know how to play with a toy. Sharon and Pauline nearly got disqualified because they had forgotten to bring a toy but Brian came to the rescue with a couple of dead rabbits he found in the office. Then it was time to go for a walk on the motorway again. There was all kinds of things we had to ignore including the squeaky pram that needed wd40 and a baby and the bike that had no chain and some real cyclists too. Andrea said that when we got back we all had to stand by our cars for inspection, so we did. Then mummy noticed that after she watched that we could load our dogs into the car then Andrea did sit next to them in the passenger seat to watch them start up the car and see if the dog was well behaved or not. Well and mummy nearly fainted, she then frantically tried to empty the contents of the passenger seat but not in time, it was so embarrassing, I didn't know where to look. When Andrea came over she went like this she went 'Kathleen, how long is it since you cleared this passenger seat? ' Mummy decided it was a rectal question and just smiled sweetly but not in such a handsome way as I can and then Andrea said 'Kathleen why is there a Santa Claus still in here it is almost April? And a Halloween mask? Is that a bucket and spade I can see down there? I can see a piece of pie and four umbrellas five coats and fourteen dog toys, there's an eccles cake too does that belong to Jennifer?' Displaying your balls in public is not a very ladylike thing to do but then I've heard your Jennifer is not very ladylike either, does it run in the family then? Mummy just smiled again. Andrea said that she had never failed anyone for being unable to sit on the passenger seat but mummy might be the first then because me and our Freya and our Jennifer had all been dead quiet like and good that she would let mummy off but just this once and only if she brought some awesome herbs with us the next time we came to her class.

Then Andrea went like this, she went 'Now I'm trying to help you out here Kathleen so I'm going to give you a clue. When we get to the questions part of the test none of the answers have 'church' in them, got it?' Then she went to the next car inspection.

It was then time for being examined by our examiner and everyone was good, even me but you see I think I gave Luna a few too many herbs from the £Sd range you see and every time Andrea came near Luna to examine her Luna thought she was a giant green spider and Luna doesn't like green things so she refused to be examined. Lynn who was being handled by Luna didn't know what to do but it was ok though because Luna let Sharon examine her instead. Lily pops who was handling Angela did her recall via the garden bench twenty yards away but she did come back! Shayla who was handling June was perfect in every way as was Helga who was handling Sharon and she was so pleased to be getting a silver medal that she kissed me in the group line-up Helga that is, not Sharon.
A special mention goes to Lottie who was handling Angela and she worked really hard to achieve the gold award.
Congratulations and well done to everyone in the Silver class of 2017

Mummy has got a lot of hard work to do over the next six weeks to get me ready for gold and Jennifer ready for bronze.

I will keep you updated on my progress.

Love Timothy. xxxx
Certified Silver and Bronze medallist 2017
P.S. I am enclosing a picture of our silver award ceremony.

Carla Lane fundraising day.
Animals in Need Spring Fayre.
Lydiate Parish Hall.

My name is Timothy Conehead the Invincible and I'm a border collie. It has been two days since my last confession.

Hello, who knows the song 'On a mountain lives a lady who she is I do not know..'? If you know the tune then you will be able to sing:- 'Pidgeons widgeons seagulls sparrows, All the birds come here to rest, but of all God's little creatures. Liverpool birds beat all the rest.'

Do you recognise the Liver birds song? It is sung by The Scaffold who are a Liverpool group and the series was written by Carla Lane who is also from Liverpool. Carla passed over to somewhere near to Rainbow Bridge in 2016 and she was dead famous. She was dead famous for her writing skills and her TV programmes and also dead famous for helping to rescue animals like amazingly handsome little me. Did I tell you that I was rescued? Well I was you see and all of the border collies who have lived in Kathleen's house of correction have been rescued just so they could come for torture training like me. I think that was why.

Anyway so anyway, you know mummy is doggist don't you, well it's only because she was handled by a border collie called Kim when she was a little girl, he was a white border collie who had been rescued and he told her that she had to keep on rescuing border collies when she grew up and so she did.

I have another question for you and it's very impotent. Did you know that it is impotent to be newted and sprayed? Well you see it's like this when deliciously handsome puppies like me grow up well they quite like to enjoy a bit of jiggy jig and have a sexy-time with a friend sometimes and this is a good thing because mummy says it is important to have fun in your life. So anyway sometimes what happens is that one of you gets pregnant and I think it's the girl and so well you see before you know it they are all born and there are more puppies than anyone can cope with all wanting to hand-glide from your neck and things and then nobody else wants them either because they are such a nuisance and poo everywhere and things and something has to be done quick.

So you see if it wasn't for all the rescue centres in the world just like Carla Lane Animals in Need then lots of us including me might not have found a loving furever home with anyone basically so because we want all of our doggy friends in rescue centres to find loving homes, even the ones who aren't border collies so it is important we all try to raise money to help them and West Lancs Canine Display team like doing this, they like doing it a lot your honour. Just so as you know I am not trying to spoil your fun, once you have been newted and sprayed you can still have a bit of jiggy jig if you can find a friend who wants fun too.

So where was I then? I know I nearly forgot to tell you about Saturday, oh it was so funny because we were all detoxing away and almost all the dogs were going roast turkey and getting everything wrong and Sharon went like this she went 'Are you responsible for the bad behaviour of these dogs today Timothy?' and I just went like this I went 'Oh most wonderful one, I have been nowhere near the herb cellar all week and the mushroom cellar is out of bounds until we have done our traffic light awareness course' and then I remembered that I wasn't supposed to mention the traffic light awareness course so I quickly went like this I went 'please ignore that last part oh wonderful one I really meant to say when we have done the herb awareness course' and she smiled at me knowingly.

Jennifer continues to persecute us all and also to learn quickly. On Sunday, oh it was really funny. Everyone was doing a recall and when it came to Mummy's turn storm Jennifer went to mummy like a magnetic bullet and then, just because she could mummy asked Jennifer to do a 'finish' and so she did. Well Brian went like this he went 'Kathleen will you please stop showing off your homework!' So mummy went like this she went 'Listen here you Brian if I want to show off my homework with Jennifer then I jolly well will ok?' and Brian went like this, he went 'but I have to pick on you Kathleen because I want to be mentioned in despatches' so mummy went 'Oh ok then' and Brian just smiled.

I was somewhere else then but someone digressed me when I wasn't looking, who was it? Come on own up?

I've got it now, I was helping to raise money for Carla Lane Animals in Need basically by just being so adorable and amazingly handsome and I was gob-smacked when I didn't win the most handsome dog competition and wanted to ask for a recount but mummy wouldn't let me. Me and our Jennifer went in for the best rescue dog competition too and we lined up next to Ethan who was handled by Dan but none of us won that one either. We will have to infiltrate the judges next time, perhaps with some of my favourite herbs..

Oh I nearly forgot to tell you, our Jennifer came second in the prettiest girl competition and Lauren who was handling Sharon wanted to take her home, I was keen for this to happen but mummy said it was my job to look after the wonder child and not Lauren's, Jennifer has apparently requested play time with Lauren at any future shows where we might meet. Just before we went home a lady called Cathy came over especially to meet me and so she could be in one of my stories because she thinks they are dead boss like, so I said ok but only if you like my stories.

As always I will keep you updated when I can,
Love Timothy. xxxx

PS. I am enclosing a picture of the handsome one with the pretty one.

April 7th 2017
Ladies Day at Aintree.
Patience and a cat.

My name is Timothy Conehead the Invincible and I'm a border collie. It has been five days since my last confession.

So it's like this you see, mummy is trying to work and Jennifer is being Jennifer and having as much fun as she can and we are trying not to help her because we are good. This is what mummy sounded like today, I recorded her and now I have inscribed the best bits for you here:-

Jennifer,
Jennifer,
Jennifer no,
No Jennifer,
No!!!
GET DOWN!
JENNIFER GET DOWN NOW!!
No,
Nooo,
Nooooo Jennifer,
Leave Laddie alone!
No!
Get down!
No Jennifer,
Jennifer get down now!
Dear Lord please send me some patience and a cat.
Where has Jennifer gone?
Jennifer NOOOOO!!!!
Oh dear God, Jennifer no!!
Down now,
Now,
DOWN!!!
NOW!!!
Mother of God and all that's holy what have you got there?

Get out of there,
Get out of there now!
Why is my phone not working?
What have you got there now?
How on earth did you get up there?
Get out of my pocket!
Where did you get that from?
Who turned the television on?
What is my welly doing on the driveway?
Oh for Pete's sake what now?
Freya will bite you if you push her too far.
Jennifer please stop emptying my plant pots out all over the drive.
Please stop stirring the drinking water up with your paw.
I'm shouting at you not reinforcing your recall!
Oh for the Love of Dogs what have you done now?
Jennifer that box was hidden underneath that stool for a reason.
Mother of God and all that's Holy Jennifer put that down NOW!
Oh that takes the biscuit that does!
That is my toe not a toy!
Where is the other half of this twenty pound note?
That parcel was waiting to be posted not unwrapped!
Why is the postman carrying my handbag up the drive?
Could you please poo on the puppy pad and not next to it?
How did you get up there?
Where has my tea gone?
Leave Timothy alone!
You are not an ornament!
Where are the TV controls?
Dear God and little fishes why me?
Jennifer watch my lips. I am trying to write!
Are you on speed?
What are my credit cards doing on the floor?
Oh Good Lord no!
Stop opening my mail!
Go near my laptop again and you will be lunch!
Laddie is not a toy he is old enough to be your great granddad,
PUT HIM DOWN NOW!
Jennifer get out of that bin!

Oh my days.
I'm sure I had a sandwich left?
Jennifer put my diary down!
Please Jennifer.
I'll shove you up a gum-tree if you don't calm down!
Get out of my bag!
That's it! I've had enough, I'm going out!
So when mummy got to the door we all wanted to make her happy
especially Jennifer so we all went and sat nicely so we could go
out with her too. Then mummy cried laughing again. I think I
should bring her something nice from one of the cellars.

I will write again soon and let you know how she gets on.
Love Timothy. xxxx

P.S. I am enclosing our latest family portrait it seems the wild child
is still growing.

Sunday 9th April 2017
Jennifer gets Bronze Day.

My name is Timothy Conehead the Invincible and I'm a border
collie, it has been two days since my last confession and I've got
bad news I'm afraid, very bad news indeed. Only Joking!!!

Oh it's just been Jennifer this and Jennifer that for the past two
days here, our Freya missed half of her lesson on Saturday so
Jennifer could have another practice at her minute have a lie down
and stay party trick which she decided to add another minute to.
Then because Freya was sick and tired of it all, well actually she
had an upset stomach and decided to throw a sickie so Jennifer got
more practice on the Sunday.

Anyway so anyway eventually and not before time I got to do my
community service but before we could do it Scott who is the
Godfather made us all stand in a circle and ordered us to all have a
mass debate in public before we could start and so we all did and
then it was written into the constitution whether we liked it or not
and any objections had to be in by midnight the night before. I
think Brian was a bit shocked but he did join in although Pauline
would have nothing to do with it and was hiding in the office and
Sharon as always just took it all in her stride. June really enjoyed it
but Wendy had had inside information so she threw a sickie too or
was that her handler Ruby? I'm not sure now. Cathy blushed and
Kate just thought it was normal behaviour for the team training
and gave me some lovely red Leicester cheese because I am just so
handsome and adorable and I noticed that Flip is rather gorgeous
too and I wondered to myself, I just wondered like this 'I wonder
when Flip gets a bit older will she like me for a boyfriend?' but
nobody noticed I was wondering so I will just have to wait and see.

We think Scott might have had the winner in the Grand National
because after a while he turned into the Crazy World of Arthur
Brown and started singing "FIRE' and all the experienced fire jump
dogs joined in and jumped through the fire hoops and were dead
boss but I wasn't too keen your honour although I did manage two

of them after the fire-brigade had been to put them out, I'm not going near the lit ones until my fire resistant outfit arrives as I wouldn't want to singe my eyebrows or anything.

I do have some really good news for you though, mummy has decided to stop swinging the lead and molly-coddling me because Lynn told her off yesterday for taking me round like a tortoise so because she managed to run I had my best ever round ever ever on the torture course and even managed to run to the end of the seesaw from Nemesis after being enticed on in the first place, oh and I'm almost fluent in the weave polls section. I got lots of lovely rewards at the end so I might do it again next week. After the torture course they brought the hula hoops out so I thought, I thought 'I know, if I jump through all of these hoops and things well I might just get more treats and cuddles.' and so I did. It was really quite fun too and we played X marks the spot as well and then Brian told mummy off for cocking her leg up when we did the reverse finish.

Anyway it was time to go home then only mummy remembered there was a test on for the Kennel Club Good Citizens Bronze Award and so she abandoned me in the chariot again and took Jennifer in to be tested.

At fifteen weeks old Jennifer Eccles was the youngest one there but because mummy has never had a puppy before she has been working really really hard with her and she was pretty dam good at everything to be fair especially her recall and have a lie down and a quick nap just for a minute exercise. She almost lost it though on the 'walk in a controlled manner' as she decided to do something she likes doing at home but has never done on the lead before and that it attack mummy's trousers and have a swing if you can. Mummy was shocked but our lovely examiner Andrea gave mummy some emergency tips on how to control the wild child in a humane manner and it was decided that she was borderline schizophrenic. No that's not right, no she is just schizophrenic. Oh no hang on Freya says she was just borderline and was having a 'I'll show mummy up' kind of moment so she was passed and given forty hours of community service to do and if she doesn't drop her Tarzan act she will have to send her certificate back. Ruby who was handling Angela and Poppy who was handling Jo also passed as did Gary with my mate Digby.

I am now in training for my Gold certificate on the 30th April and I will keep you updated on my progress.
Love Timothy. xxxx

Jennifer gains her bronze award.

9th April 2017

P.S I am enclosing a picture the bronze child with her certificate age 14 weeks old..

My name is Timothy Conehead the Invincible and I'm a border collie. It has been five days since my last confession and we have a Trump Wall.

So you see it's like this, we have a trump wall that keeps us all here against our free will at Love House and there is a big long white trump wall and two different hedge trump walls that are really old and thick and have been keeping border collies imprisoned here since mummy moved here in the olden days.

The hedges are impenetrable and then we have the big Shankly gates that have an extra lock on just for safe keeping. When I say the hedges are impenetrable what I really mean is that they used to be impenetrable,

It was like this your honour, mummy was playing with herself on the intersex and we had been thrown out and abandoned in the cold.. Mummy can see most of us and the gate when she is playing with herself and so she was quite happy. What mummy didn't see was that the wild child had climbed up onto the little wall behind the hedge and was playing at being a miner you see.

What happened was when Sir Lord Jack was here he used to have three big deep holes in the back garden and one of them he shared with Laddie the Baddie and that one is still there. So when mummy wasn't looking yesterday I was showing the wild child how much fun she could have if she dug herself an escape route and I was thinking that if she did then I could fill it in later and no one would know. So I digressed myself then just so you understood, so there we were imprisoned by the trump wall and abandoned in the cold when Jennifer decided to practice digging an escape route next to the front trump wall hedge and so while she was digging away at her tunnel she somehow found that she had penetrated the impenetrable trump wall hedge and was on the wrong side of the Shankly Gates. So I went like this I went 'Run Jennifer run, escape now while you can. Someone is bound to like you if you keep trying, go on run quickly before you get told off, I won't tell mummy anything just run run run' The wild child however has decided that she quite likes it here and started to cry and squeak and make a terrible noise demanding to be allowed back in to our prison.

Meanwhile the mummy was quite happy playing with herself until she suddenly heard the wild child crying in her panicky way and she rushed out to find her on the wrong side of our impenetrable trump wall and so she had to not panic or swear and open the extra lock on the Shankly Gates so she could let the little whinge back in.

We had go on an emergency message to the get it done yourself shop to buy some chicken wire, we think mummy is going to build her a chicken run in the back garden to keep her safe. In the mean time we have had our play area reduced greatly as the extendable play pen we keep her in sometimes has been extended to cut off most of the driveway so we cannot reach the trump wall hedges. I'll have to think of another way to help the Bronze child to escape..
I will keep you updated as soon as I know more.

Love Timothy. xxxx
P.S. I am enclosing a picture that clearly shows the bronze child stalking me, please send help.

16th April 2017
Easter Sunday.
Flower Child Blooms.

My name is Timothy Conehead the Invincible and I'm a border collie. It has been two days since my last confession.

I haven't had a minutes peace here running around after this lot and it's supposed to be a nice peaceful weekend.

So it was like this you see storm Jennifer who shows no sign of blowing out although she does enough blowing off to make her own trump wall, well so she was playing zoomies and squeakies and squealies and mummy thought 'I know, if I just close the childproof safety gate with Jennifer the other side of it just to keep me and Laddie safe for a while then Freya and Timothy can babysit for me and I can get some work done' and so she did.

The thing is you see mummy keeps bringing boxes home and I'm not sure if she is planning to post her somewhere or not but she lets her play with the boxes just to get used to being in one. So when there was a lot of noise of boxes being moved around the mummy wasn't too concerned and she just carried on working. After a little while she decided to come and check whether we were babysitting the wild child properly and when she looked around the door she went a funny colour and I think she nearly fainted your honour.

What had happened you see was Jennifer had decided to help mummy with the gardening again, did you know she likes helping mummy by emptying the plant posts out on the driveway? Well she especially likes emptying all the plant pots out and she thinks the trowel is her personal property and often carries it around with her, we think she is into flower power, well she is into some sort of power anyway.

So where was I then? Oh yes I know, she brought a plant pot into the hallway for mummy and then she brought the trowel in and then she thought 'I know I'm sure mummy would like it if I watered some of her plants while she is keeping Laddie safe from me' and so Jennifer the intrepid explorer went and found mummy's pink watering can which she always up until now keeps water in and she dragged it down the driveway and into the hallway. The noises mummy could hear that she thought were cardboard boxes were the pink watering can being dragged around the hallway. Every time it was dragged a bit more water came out so when mummy decided to come and see if we were being responsible babysitters you can understand how she nearly fainted when she saw the hallway was nearly flooded with a plant pot and accessories floating around. Mummy didn't have any shoes on either you see just socks and so she had to take her socks off so she could paddle through the hall to get her wellies and to get a mop and to secure the wild child in a humane way.

I will keep you informed of any further developments.
Love Timothy. xxxx

I am enclosing exhibit A your honour which shows clearly the wild child caught red handed wit the pink watering can and the flood. You can clearly see my good self and our Freya behind her looking innocent and helpless as to what to do with her.

23rd April 2017 St Georges Day.
The Wrong Trousers.
My name is Timothy Conehead the Invincible and I'm a border collie it has been three days since my last confession.

After the devastation of storm Jennifer and the planting up of the hallway last week I was looking forward to going west for a rest. I say west but what I mean is the training school where I do my community service.

I was a bit confused when we were being loaded into the chariot as Freya wasn't loaded in with me, she was left at home in charge of Laddie the Baddie who is getting slower but coping really well with the bullying from the wild child.

I discovered that because the mummy has been doing lots of homework on the tiny terrorist and because she is learning quick Sharon wanted to put her through her paces in the big girls class to see if she was up to silver standard and apparently she is. I am unclear your honour how someone who is so naughty is also apparently so clever.

Misty's is a very big German who also handles June and Jennifer is Misty's best friend, Misty doesn't have many friends she eats most of them, I must ask her if I can interest her in a nice bottle of Chianti from mummy's cellar. Anyway Jennifer stands next to Misty in class I think she is Misty's minder now.

So anyway Brian arrived for training only half dressed on Saturday, when I say half dressed what I mean is he only had half of his uniform on now I'm not sure if matron threw him out before he could get dressed properly or it could be that Pauline who owns him has washed his trousers on a boil wash or it could be that she has sold them I'm not sure except that he definitely had the wrong trousers on.

Jennifer heard Brian and Sharon saying that they were bringing the cats in for training on Sunday but we don't think they are going to be any good at well anything really.

Shayla has finally managed to train June to get her to do her emergency stop in the right place, I told her how to do it when we were having a quickie in the cellar but don't tell anyone will you. I'm just amazingly handsome, oh sorry I meant to say that I'm just amazingly good at the emergency stop but I am very handsome too of course.

On Saturday I was abandoned for half an hour while mummy disappeared with June and so was Shayla, I think these trainers need reporting I mean how would they like to be abandoned and isolated with no one to love them for half an hour? I was so miffed I hid in the grass so mummy nearly couldn't find me when she finally came back. Wendy had to tell her where I was. It seems that if we are good and don't whinge or cry when our humans disappear for half an hour then it makes us gold standard, allegedly.

On Sunday we did more practicing for our exams next week and then we did the torture course and I got all the way around without any help from anyone until we got to the killer seesaw and then Sharon helped and I did do it again and didn't faint or anything and finished with the weave polls which I get better at every time I do them.

Next it was time for the hoola hoop training and I was fabulous at everything apart from having a jump with Shayla, I'd rather wait for her to come back to the cellar with me.

It was time to go home then and all the team decided to take Brian back to the old peoples home and just to cheer him up they took some of the equipment with them to put on a display just for him and Matron, wasn't that really nice of them. I hope he remembers to put the right trousers on next time.

I will keep you updated on events when I can.
Love Timothy. xxxx

Jennifer's a girl.

My name is Timothy Conehead the Invincible and I'm a border collie. It has been three days since my last confession.

Oh I'm all confused your honour and a bit excited too. Did you know that Jennifer's a girl? You see it's like this, I thought Jennifer was a cat but then we got playing and she thought she would hitch a lift and so I just decided to eject her and then she was rolling on the floor laughing. I just thought 'I know, I'll just play with the cat a bit longer' so I did and then she was just lying there with her belly on show and everything and I just noticed that she wasn't a boy and she must be a girl and I was a bit surprised and so I looked again just to check and I was definitely right and so I kept looking just to be sure and I had a sniff as well and I thought "I wonder if mummy has noticed that I have noticed that Jennifer is a girl" and I did look at the mummy and I could see that she had noticed that I had noticed that Jennifer was a girl. So I thought, I thought "I hope mummy hasn't noticed what I'm thinking yet or it will be ten years hard labour for me if she has" So I just smiled sweetly in a superbly handsome sort of way that only I can and wondered about how much fun I might be having with Jennifer in the future...

I will keep you informed of any further discoveries I may make..
Love Timothy. xxxx

My name is Timothy Conehead the Invincible and I'm a border collie and it has been four days since my last confession.

I have good news and bad news I'm afraid your honour, very bad news indeed. Well it's like this you see I've been so excited to discover Jennifer was a girl and thinking of how I can talk Shayla into allowing me to have a harem you see but I don't think June would be very happy and so I think I may have got the herbs wrong this week.

It's just been all go because we had our exams and we have been practicing hard all week and mummy was certain I would be getting gold and not certain that the wild child would get silver and she was wrong.

When mummy arrived for training on Saturday Sharon went like this she went 'what is that instrument of torture you are using on Jennifer this week Kathleen?' and mummy went like this she went 'I'll be using your chastity belt if this doesn't work Sharon, or is it Brian's?' Sharon just smiled and hoped mummy didn't realise it was her who had entered our chariot in for the 'Most rubbish in a car' competition. Anyway the straight jacket that mummy had put on Jennifer seemed to be working and the wild child walked properly up and down the identity parade apart from when she stopped to give Riley a kiss. She did really well in her rehearsals and aced the agility. I heard somebody saying that she was better than Timothy but there must be another Timothy only I haven't met him yet because she is too young and too little and like a cat to be better than me.

So where was I then? Oh yes Brian told me off for telling people he wore the wrong trousers and apparently he only has three pair altogether in the world and if the other pair get dirty as well then he will be coming in as a commando and apparently that is not a pretty site. He was telling me about his holidays too and this year he is looking forward to going to Muchslapping in the Dell, I hope he takes photographs while he is there, I think it is in the bush country but I'm not sure.

I was really quite good in team training but still refuse to have a jump with Shayla in front of everyone. Sharon asked mummy if she thought I might follow Jennifer across the see-saw, I didn't know our Jennifer could do the see-saw, someone said she flies across it like the black panther. I told you she was a cat. Poppy who handles Jo and Lou whichever one she is in the mood for really, well she was feeling a bit hungry and ate mummy's treats out if her pocket and they were still in the bag. Jo said her poo came out wrapped the next day.

So anyway after team training and a quick banana it was time for the silver test and Jennifer went for a walk on the motorway, she said it was really scary and she saw a headless horseman who was with Dick Turpin, several monks were making green wine and singing sea shanty's and there were Blue Meanies everywhere and she thinks she also saw Lord Lucan but she's not sure. When she got back in Andrea told her to stand by the chariot and wait for inspection so she did you see and when Andrea arrived she bribed her with a Werthers original just so she wouldn't say anything about how messy it was even though it had been tidied by mummy. Our Jennifer aced everything else even the two minute 'down stay' and so she passed you see with honours, well not really with honours because I don't think they do them but if they did she would have got them of that I'm certain your honour. So at still just seventeen weeks old and still looking like a cat Jennifer Eccles passed her Kennel Club Silver Good Citizens Award with just a tiny bit of help from the mummy. Congratulations to the others who passed silver including Ethan and Luna and Hazel and Jess, and Chris and Millie well done to all of you.

Then it came to my Gold test and we went out for another walk on the motorway. There was no sign of Dick Turpin but I did see a horse drawn coach being driven by a headless driver but then I noticed it was just Brian showing off. Sharon had told Wendy earlier that it was too cold to be stripping off today and she couldn't take it anyway after all the complaints from the last time and so she had to mind the baby but she wasn't very happy about it and she walked along the motorway bouncing the poor baby up and down until it was sea-sick. June chaperoned mummy and Ethan just in case they talked too much and didn't concentrate properly or anything, especially mummy who got told off for walking too fast. We didn't have to do chariot inspection for gold, Andrea said she had seen enough of the chariot to last a lifetime. I was pretty good at everything else and excellence itself at being sent away for a lie down and forty winks., I even brought my own bed. Then came the two minute 'down stay' at which I have excelled at over the last few months in that very same spot and the last part mummy goes into the polygamy tunnel for a quickie with everyone else for a half a minute and I am just so good at it. Now I'm not sure why I decided to get up when mummy disappeared because we do this exercise lots of times and I never move an inch, it could be because I got the munchies but I'm not sure. Anyway no second chances were given for that exercise and so your honour I am afraid to tell you that unfortunately I failed my gold exam. Congratulations to Sharon, June and Jodie who passed and commiserations to Brian and Lynn who will be in the handsome lineup with me for our next attempt, mummy say's she will bring the hammer and nails and some very special herbs and a blindfold for Andrea, just to make sure we all pass. I have to get my gold before the wild child or I will be overthrown and everything.

Our Laddies says it's not fair and when are they having a class and awards for the golden oldies.

I am enclosing exhibit A your honour The Wild Child receiving her Silver award age 17 weeks.

I will work hard and write again soon.

Love Timothy. xxxx

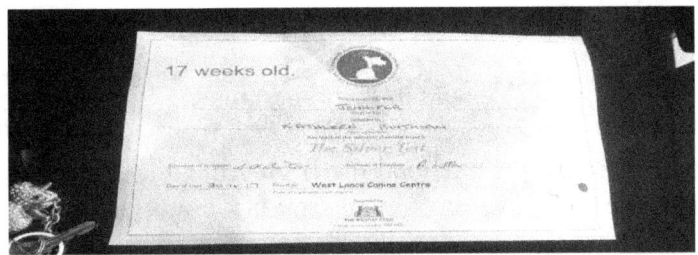

17 weeks old.

Wednesday 3rd May 2017

Yes we have no bananas..

My name is Timothy Conehead the Invincible and I'm a border collie. It has been three days since my last confession.

I have some really shocking news to report your honour, shocking. It's like this you see, did you know that bananas are good for you? Well mummy says they are and they have potassium in them for your heart kidneys brain and muscles, they also contain 5HTP which gets converted to serotonin in your brain and makes you smile and be happy without having to visit the herb cellar. Mummy says it is really important to keep your serotonin levels up especially when you are being handled by four border collies. She says they are the answer to almost everlasting life.

Every single day mummy has a banana for her breakfast and she says it's good to get your mouth around something firm and fruity to start off your day. We all get some too, mummy saves us all a small piece everyday so as we will live almost forever and we all like it especially Jennifer. Laddie is sixteen and a half tomorrow and he has banana every single day and so did Sir Lord Jack who lived to be eighteen.

Mummy keeps the bananas hanging from the vegetable basket on a hook out of everybody's way. When I say out of everybody's way what I mean is that never in the past hundred years has any single border collie even ever thought about trying to take something that is hanging up there. Not until today that is.

Unfortunately mummy couldn't have her 5HTP today because the wild child decided she wanted to be high on serotonin and needed some extra energy and so she stole the bananas. The Crime Prevention Officer is calling around to have a word with Jennifer later today after mummy has been shopping for some more.

I will keep you updated on the crime scene as much as I can.

Love Timothy. xxxx

P.S. I am enclosing exhibit A your honour which shows clearly the wild child caught in the act.

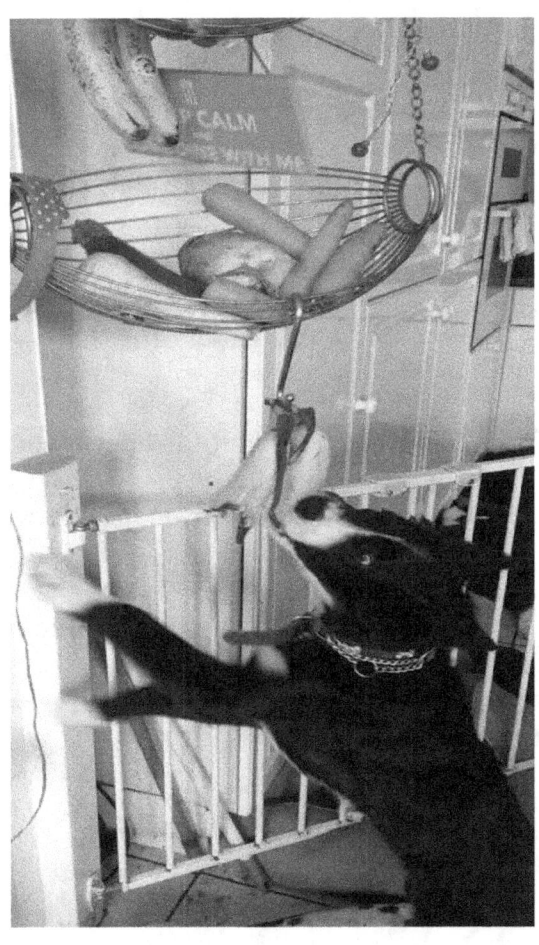

My name is Timothy Conehead the Invincible and I'm a border collie it has only been one day since my last confession.

Oh dear, does anyone know what an erection is please? Is it that excited feeling you get and after the climax you have a trump?

Did you know that there are erections all over the place today?

Well there are they are everywhere you look and they make some people smile and they make some people flustered and they make some people out of breath but mummy just takes them all in her stride.

Mummy says that if there is an erection near you and you don't do anything about it then you can't complain when the inflatable goes down or anything really.

Voting in an erection can be a labour of love or if you don't care about anyone but yourself you might put a cross on a condom or something, I think that's what mummy said but I'm not sure.

Some people love erections and some people just think they are a waste of time and some people just go off them. I think mummy likes them because she talks about them a lot and says we should have them more often like weekly or something I think. Don't tell her I told you will you?

Love Timothy. xxxx

Friday 5th May 2017

Laddie the Baddie's Obituary.

I am so very sad to tell you that the lovely Laddie the Baddie has gone to join Sir Lord Jack at the Bridge. He was 16 and a half yesterday and a very sprightly old codger he was too.

I was asked to foster Laddie by a local rescue but it was over a year before I realised they had given him to me for free 'because nobody ever looked at him' He was the third dog brought in by a lady who got them as puppies but then didn't know what to do with them.

He wasn't house trained and on his first night with me he did five big stinky poos in my bedroom, I wasn't impressed. It didn't take me too long to house train him but for a collie he was slow to learn other tricks. He was noise activated and would go mental when the microwave beeped, when you opened or closed the door of the microwave, when you opened the freezer [the fridge it seems was fine] when you turned the taps on in the bath and so on. He sometimes had to be locked out of the kitchen when I was cooking as he would suddenly lunge at you if you were using a 'noisy' piece of equipment. Putting petrol in the car was hysterical as he wanted to kill the invader and woe betide me if I had the car washed with him inside. I used to worry the windows would go. Noises frighten Timothy but they made Laddie want to attack it.

It was quite funny because every single dog I brought home while I had Laddie would pick on him, I had to give Scampi his own ball to keep in his mouth while we were out because he wanted to get Laddie. Laddie was never fazed by any of them he was a cocky little sod who always had to have the last word.

I went to work one very hot summers day and left a front bedroom window open but I didn't close the safety gate across the door or did I? My neighbour decided to mow her lawn [Laddie liked to kill lawn mowers too and would jump up and down like a pogo stick trying to get over our fence to kill it] and as she wheeled it out she heard Laddie barking looked up and saw him at the open window! She was terrified he would jump out so as slowly as she could manage took the mower back out of sight. I never did that again.

He was hopeless but in an adorable way, if there was ever any trouble going down you could be sure Laddie was there. He stole food at every given opportunity and I remember coming home from work late one night fancying something on toast only to discover Laddie had eaten the entire loaf. I settled for a bag of crisps.

I was on a course in Hungerford one year and Pauline minded the boys for me, Laddie allegedly stole a whole piece of ham from a pan on the cooker, he was apparently found half way up the garden eating it. He denied all knowledge of course.

One time I was at the Marina, we were playing in the lake long before it became infested with strange algae. We were having a great time throwing the ball in for them to swim out to and bring back but then I looked up and saw a couple of mounted policemen. Oh flip, I thought. or words to that effect, I had Jack, Laddie, Lady and Scampi at the time and they all liked rounding up moving objects. I could see me being locked up for police harassment, my life passed before my eyes. I had no ball as I had just thrown it in and it was floating in the middle. I called them and legged it back to the chariot and as they each jumped in I counted only three. I looked back, no sign of anyone. I counted again and realised it was Laddie who was missing but he was nowhere to be seen. I legged it back to the lake and could see the ball floating but no Laddie and then I spotted him, it was too steep for him to climb out and he was hanging onto the side not wanting to leave his precious ball. I hauled him out unceremoniously and managed to get the ball.

There was another time on Formby beach years ago when we used to go every day, some horses came galloping down the beach so I legged onto the sand dunes and into the woods knowing all four would follow, Laddie was the last to join me that day. I remember when Laddie came training with me, he would always stop in the tunnels and eat whatever cat poo he could find, he did get out of that in time but to begin with his outside eating habits were just gross.

He did know all the basic commands especially recall the most important one in my opinion. When Freya and Timothy Conehead came along and I began training with them it was so funny as both Jack and Laddie clearly remembered their training and as I would call the two new ones and give them a sweetie when they responded, the two old codgers arrived for sweeties too and remembered a 'touch' on my hand may bring a sweetie too. I had to readjust their food intake to allow for all these extra treats. Whatever I would ask the new ones to do the old codgers obliged too. When you are teaching new things it is advisable to train your dogs separately of course but when you are all out together and you are reinforcing recall, you just have to reward them all.

Laddie had vestibular last May and I thought I had lost him then but he got over it, it returned this January and again he survived it and was being given his meds on a weekly basis. By the end of February I asked for his meds to be put back to monthly and he plodded on as before.

When Jennifer arrived he wasn't too pleased, Laddie like Jack has had to put up with quite a number of new arrivals both short term and long term but he has never encountered a puppy before. She was bad to him and she knew he was infirm and played on it so I never left them alone.

Most of my Golden Oldies have developed arthritis and Laddie was no exception and he has been slowing up for sometime now but while you are still eating and enjoying going for walks then there is still a decent quality of life, being able to run isn't everything. This last week Laddie seemed to almost seize up and collapsed a few times. He was struggling with our walks and he came and sat with me of an evening instead of staying on his own couch, he knew it was time to let go. .

I would have loved to take him to our special place in the pinewoods but he would have struggled too much so we have just had lots of cuddles and I explained that it was time for him to join the others and how much I would miss him. We had a banquet this morning in the garden of cheese and sausages and freshly cooked chicken breast and of course rib-eye steak and he we even let the poorly fed dogs have some too, not the rib-eye steak though that was just for my Laddie. Timothy will have to look to Jennifer now to learn how to be a baddie.

I took him today after morning surgery and Rob came out to him as he lay quite happily in the back of our chariot, he agreed he had been valiant and had fought enough. Rob gave him his injection to send him to sleep and I talked to Laddie and sang to him as it took effect, then Rob gave him his final injection and he slipped away. I have lost my two old codgers just nine months apart , I have had them for so long and am grateful for that time but I can't imagine life now without them.

R.I.P. my naughty one, please give my Jack a big kiss from me and wait patiently for mummy, there are thirteen collies waiting for me now and one day you can all stampede me and we will cross the Bridge together.
All things must pass and today I lost my Laddie.
❤

Circle of Life.

On Friday 5th May2017 my heart that had never really healed since losing my Sir Lord Jack nine moths earlier was wrenched open again as I had to let my Laddie go too.
I understand why some people will only ever have one dog because they refuse to put themselves through the pain of losing another. That pain, the void that follows is almost unbearable. Highly sensitive people feel more deeply than others and I am one of them and at times like this of course I wish I wasn't but the flip side is you also feel the ecstasy and the love and the humour more than the average person too which is why I have had so many collies no doubt. The need to rescue is enormous as is the need to feel loved and I invariably find myself with another usually within the year.

I didn't want to go back to training after I lost Laddie, I just wanted the world to stop and feel my pain but of course it doesn't stop not for me not for anyone. It is a cycle and it will continue forever at least until the Earth stops spinning, the circle of life. Laddies time had come and was now gone, just like Jacks nine months earlier. I wondered how many more years of community service I still had to do before I could rejoin my beautiful collies with their unconditional love and mischievousness. They say that we choose to come here and moreover they say we choose to live the lives we have, hmm. No comment.

Grieving was different this time because now I had Jennifer, silver medalist and wild child extraordinaire. I had convinced myself that she was somehow sent from Jack to lift me and never having had a puppy before she was and still is an eye opener. On the Sunday, two days after losing Laddie I was having a cry while the little ones were playing out on the driveway. I was only crying quietly when Jennifer appeared and leapt at me kissing my tears away followed closely by Timothy who helped to make sure there were no tears left. The little ones were not going to let me stay in that dark lonely place where I can sometimes end up staying for months. I would have to work harder at picking myself up this time.

Before Laddie passed I was in the process of getting things in order so as I could edit 'Community Service' with a view to publishing in time for my birthday on the 4th June. I had already realised that I was putting myself under too much pressure to have it published by then but surely I could manage it for soon after, perhaps Timothy's birthday on the 18th June? I like to have special dates to remember things by, I never start things on a Monday I start them on the nearest special date that comes along. There are lots of special dates in my life and because they are special it gives me more encouragement when attempting new goals.
It didn't have to be published but I knew some people were waiting eagerly for it. Looking at Jennifer dragging a piece of hose pipe into my living room [I'm guessing she thought her plants pots, which were also in the room, needed watering] I acknowledged the fact that I had been given this beautiful mischievous border collie to mould and fashion and if I stopped her training now I knew I would regret it later. Jennifer wasn't planned although for years I have been saying things like 'one day I'll have a puppy brand new to me and it will come from a rescue centre.' So perhaps the Universe has been waiting for just the right moment to make that happen for me. I would have to work really hard on myself and get the kids back to school. So with tears running down my face I began to write Timothy's obituary on Laddie, life is for the living and it must go on. . R.I.P. My naughty boy. ❤

My name is Timothy Conehead the Invincible and I'm a border collie, it has been just one day since my last confession.

I have some really sad news to tell you, our Laddie the Baddie has had enough and has followed in Sir Lord Jacks footsteps and gone to Rainbow Bridge for a rest.

He came to me on Thursday you see and he went like this, he went 'Look here Timothy mummy has been telling me I was thick since I arrived here all those years ago and I might be the odd butty short of a picnic but even I know the difference between an election and an erection. Try asking our Freya she'll put you straight just don't go near her with one though or she'll eat you, she's not fond of elections of any kind.' and then he went like this 'Anyway I've had enough of your silly stories and I can't be doing with this wild child Jennifer the cat thing that keeps attacking me and sitting on my head and then smiles sweetly and innocently when mummy is looking.' then he went for a lie down.

Later on when mummy had gone to find where the local erection was he told me that from tomorrow I was to be the mummy's right hand man and I had to look after her and comfort her when she was sad. He said that because we are so full of energy and cleverness and naughtiness, unconditional love and sometimes wisdom but not me that we just use our bodies up quicker than the two legged ones. This means we don't get to stay here very long and our mummy's or daddy's get really very sad when we have to go. He said that some people need minding a bit more than other people and that is why they seem to have more dogs. Laddie has promised to pop back every so often just like Sir Lord Jack does just to check that we are minding mummy properly and stuff and that I had to be brave and not be frightened of noises. He also said I should look for an on-line course on the intersex if I was going to continue with my blogs or find mummy's dictionary and use it.

The next day we all had a picnic together in our garden and I asked Laddie if he had a special request for his last meal and he said he wanted salmon on croot, so I cooked him some salmon but I still can't find the croot shop so I hope they have some at Rainbow Bridge. Then mummy took Laddie on his last message and he never came back Mummy says he is still here really just like all the others are but we just don't have quite so much dog hair to clean up. Mummy says that we are all made of energy and some of us have too much but that energy never dies but our bodies do so we have to leave our bodies here and just take all our energy to the next part of our adventure and behave ourselves as well.

I wonder if our Laddie is going to be canonised like Sir Lord Jack, I think he might have been a bit too naughty for that but I'm not sure.

Mummy says that all things must pass and even though it makes us really sad when we lose a loved one we should also see it as a new beginning. New beginnings always follow endings whether they were sad or not and we should always be working hard to make somebody happy, even Jennifer the Cat.

I will try and write again soon.
Love Timothy. xxxx
P.S. I am enclosing exhibit A your honour which we think is mummy's favourite picture of Laddie the Baddie and if you look carefully you can see Love House behind him. He looks like he was probably being very good that day but I'm sure he wasn't.

The Killer See-saw Conquered Day.

My name is Timothy Conehead the Invincible and I'm a border collie. It has been just over one week since my last confession.

Mummy has been really sad because Laddie the Baddie hasn't been here to shout at or anything and she didn't really want to go back to training but we persuaded her to as we don't want Jennifer the Cat to be wild for ever and she needs to be disciplined and stuff.

Mummy nearly didn't go but then she did and Super Sharon came to see if she was alright and mummy whinged a bit and Super Sharon went like this she went 'Kathleen you just need to keep busy, now come on and I'll whip you into shape.' and then she whizzed around fast just like Wonder Woman and when she stopped whizzing she was dressed in black leather and had this big long whip and she cracked that whip and mummy ran quickly into class and did as she was told and even listened properly and everything just so she wouldn't get whipped again.

There weren't many people there this weekend and lots of them have run away to Scotland again and we think they've gone to live in a commune where they all dance naked around the campfire of a night but we're not sure.

Anyway so anyway we were all very good except me who failed the Gold rehearsal 'sit quiet and don't move while mummy goes into the polygamy tunnel for a quickie' test. Mummy's theory about the gate not being closed for the test was thrown out and so now she is going to decide which glue to use and she has heard that fixident is pretty good so she might try that.

Freya was her normal charming 'don't look at me like that or I'll have you' narky self who settled down and did everything in slow motion. Everyone think Freya is old and slow but when we run on the haven she is the fastest of us all.

Jennifer the cat must have found my stash of speed in the illegal herb cellar as she did everything at supersonic speed and then went 'what next?'

Jennifer was allowed into the Advanced class on Saturday and I'm not sure why your honour, the only thing she is advanced in is thuggery, villainy and destruction. Ask mummy to tell you about what she did to the pressure cooker lid, on second thoughts don't, it only makes her cry. Anyway I did the display team course but when we got to the killer seesaw Jennifer was there and they took Jennifer across the seesaw and then me and then they did it again. So the next day when it was my turn to do it again I went over the see-saw with just mummy and some treats and nobody had to help. It was quite nice really and everybody clapped so I might just do it again. I was so pleased with myself that I even had a quick jump with Shayla and I jumped Luna too for the first time ever and I did all the hoops right and everything and Lynn and June and Super Sharon all think I'm improving really well since they had Jennifer in to show me up. I'm going to have to try really hard now.

Oh I nearly forgot to tell you when Jennifer was in the Advanced class Helga told her she wasn't old enough to be in the class and Jennifer started to cry and so Shayla who is my first true love that mummy doesn't know about because she isn't a border collie well yes that one, so Shayla went like this to Helga she went 'listen here you Helga Jennifer is my mate and I'll have you if you pick on her again ok? ' but before Helga could say 'ok Shayla, well does my bum look big in this collar then?' Luna decided to defend Jennifer too and I just shouted 'Fight! Fight!' Oh there was blood everywhere and guts and stuff and the paramedics had to be called in and everything – only joking!! Super Sharon soon sorted it out and everyone got added extra hours to their community service. I think they might have been fighting over me you know as I am just so handsome and adorable.

Ben was absent from team training as I believe Wendy has enrolled him on an art course as he enjoys painting so much.

I would just like to wish Leo a happy 6th birthday on the 16th May this week he is a big lad and we have eaten the lovely treats his mummy Lynn brought in for us already so thank you very much.

I will write soon and keep you informed of my progress.
Love Timothy. xxxx
I am enclosing exhibit A your honor which clearly shows how brilliant we all are in the Advanced class, except for Jennifer the cat who wasn't meant to be there.

My name is Timothy Conehead the Invincible and I'm a border
collie. It has been seven days since my last confession.

Oh it is just terrible here your honour and we may need some help.
Mummy is really sad because our Laddie has gone to join Sir Lord
Jack and I know she tries really hard not to but she cries. Me and
Freya and Jennifer the cat work really hard at kissing all those tears
away for her though and I know she really appreciates it and she
really likes it when Jennifer brings her presents to cheer her up too.
I think she feels really lucky to have us and she keeps saying 'Just
my luck and why am I so lucky and why me, why me.'

After mummy came back from taking Laddie on his final message
she took me to the herb cellar and she went like this she went
'Timothy you are now the man of the house, my right hand man.
You are my Head Boy and in charge of the girls.' and then she
went 'With this title comes great responsibility grasshopper and I
hope you remember everything Sir Lord Jack taught you as you
will need to be perfect if you are to be my Head Boy. Can you do
this for me Timothy?

I just smiled in a very handsome but alarmed sort of way and I just
thought like this I thought 'How can I be in charge of our Freya
and Jennifer the cat when the both of them keep picking in me?'
and then I thought ' I don't think mummy has noticed that Jennifer
the cat is bullying me but if I'm Head Boy maybe she will stop it'
and then I just gave mummy a big hug and lots of kisses and
another hug. Then I wondered and when I was wondering I went
like this I went 'I'll have to get Sir Lord Jack to stay longer on his
next visit as I'm not a bit sure about this 'being perfect' business but
he will know and he might know who the grasshopper is too' Then
I went to have a play with myself.

Anyway so anyway we have been doing lots of training this week
and mostly having a lie down on a mat training and our Jennifer is

dead boss like, she is almost as good as me on this one and she's only twenty weeks old! So when we went for torture training this week Pauline was talking to some new puppy people and she went like this she went 'I can remember most of the dogs names but not the people apart from the ones I can't get rid of like Kathleen here' and then she went like this ' Jennifer I was really impressed with your having a lie down on your mat training I saw the other night on the intersex so I'm going to put you in charge of the puppy pen as you seem to have assumed that role anyway. Could you give my Brian some tips please before I put him back in the old peoples home for the night?' Our Jennifer just smiled and continued to round up the other puppies, well somebody has got to do it haven't they?

Our Freya was telling me that there is a lady called Tess who is owned by a border collie called Marvin, I've got a big brother with two legs called Marvin but he lives a long way away and it's a long time since he has been home now and I hope he comes to meet Jennifer soon. In Freya's class Brian said he was going to get the old girl out to get her some training but that the class was too big, I don't think that is a very nice way to speak about Pauline, do you?

Anyway so when it was my class I stood next to my mate Jet who owns Brian and when it was his turn to do the emergency stop he turned on an angle and said to me he went 'Timothy me old mate, can you take me home with you so as your Jennifer can teach me how to go away for a lie down please? Me owl fellah has forgotten how to do it and we've got the Gold test coming up again soon.'
I went like this, I went 'Jet me old mate our Jennifer has an IQ of 180 and she'll be running the country in a few years you mark my words, I'll sneak you into the back of the chariot when no one is looking mate.' and then I had a think about it and I went like this I went ' Jet don't you think your owl fellah will get a cob on if Jennifer teaches you how to have a lie down mate, him being a trainer and everything?' and Jet thought about it, I could see he was thinking about it because he looked confused. Then Jet went like this he went ' Timothy mate, he might throw a wobbler if you write

about it in your bog mate that your Jennifer is training me and he might repel you' and then he went to have a play with himself and another think and when he came back he went 'I don't think he will repel you you know because if he did he wouldn't be in anymore of your bogs would he? He likes being mentioned in dispatches Timothy so lets go for it mate.' We couldn't sneak him out this week but we will do it soon your honour as we are both going for Gold quite soon with our mate Luna.

Sharon was telling mummy about how she only gets a bath on a Thursday and now she can't even do that because the washer has broken her tap and won't fix it, and she couldn't be Super Sharon this week because the washer has also shrunk her costume and washed away her magnetic personality and everything. I think that's what she said but I might be wrong.

Jennifer was for some strange reason brought into the team training class this week and she soon seemed to get the hang of the weave hoops and when it came to the tunnel hoops she ran through them like super sonic the hedgehog while I was left abandoned unwanted and unloved like tails the fox, just tied to a beach languishing away like anything. I think she has been going to Andreas class where I used to go to learn to think with my mind. I'm really not very happy with this and may need to take drastic action.

I nearly forgot to tell you there was murder on Sunday! When I say murder what I mean is Wendy had this big stick and she was going to beat Ruby with it but Sharon stepped in right away and she went like this she went 'I'll have none of that in my class thank you very much Wendy' and then proceeded to beat Digby's dad with it but it was in an orderly fashion your honour.

I will keep you updated on our progress your honour just as soon as I can.

Love Timothy. xxxx

My name is Timothy Conehead the Invincible and I'm a border collie. It has been one week since my last confession.

It was so hot on Saturday your honour that our teachers had no clothes on, when I say they had no clothes on what I mean is that they said it was far too hot for their black uniform and so Super Sharon wore a pretty pink number and Brian wore a red Tshirt appealing for spare parts. Apparently he was born in 1855 and his working parts all now need replacing, Pauline said that matron was going to look through the spare parts cupboard later but if anyone had any spare bits they could offer she would be very grateful.

Our Freya continues to be a nark, we think she is going through a midlife crisis especially as she has just realised that she is the oldest girlie in the pack now and next in line for fine dining. I think she is hoping that Jennifer graduates from puppy school soon so as she can retire and dream about Angus Aberdeen mince, braised steak with seasonal vegetables and salmon on croot. She moves so slow in class that people think she is really old but one day I'll post a video on YouTube to show you how fast she really is.

So then it was my turn to sunbathe on the training field Lou who belongs to Jo and Poppy decided to be the doorman and demanded to see id from everyone as they came in only mummy didn't have any so she went like this she went 'Just listen hear Kathleen, if you don't want to be barred for life them you have to arrive here tomorrow with a blue shell paddling pool for our Poppy or you won't be allowed in again. So mummy just went like this she went 'Oh ok but I might have to have a word with my friend Anna who is also a doorman to see if you are allowed to demand paddling pools for menaces ok?' Lou just smiled and let us in and then I was just superbly handsome as usual and perfect at being sent away for a quick lie down and quite magnificent at being bribed to do almost anything mummy asked me to really. Then it all went badly wrong. Mummy decided to go and bring our Jennifer the cat in to show me how to do the seesaw and she decided to attach my lead to the open gate and abandon me there while she went for the wild child. I decided to move but when I moved the gate moved and I thought it was going to turn into the killer gate and I'd already fought off a killer jump that day so I panicked. Luckily for me Lynn saw me and then Wendy did too and they came and rescued me and played with me so I wouldn't be totally traumatised and then they told mummy off. Aunty Rita was there to give me some special big hugs though so I was alright then. After that Jennifer showed me how to do the seesaw but I still wasn't convinced until Sharon arrived with the red Leicester cheese and so I did it for her then.

Mummy didn't want to be barred for life and as Anna is in Thailand for the foreseeable future she thought it was best to go and buy a paddling pool for Poppy and she got one for Jennifer too. Me and our Freya the Hunter are far too cool to be playing in water so we got a new tuggy toy and some sweeties.

On our way to school the next day our chariot malfunctioned and mummy had to do an emergency pit-stop on the motorway and fix it quick, she was late for school and Brian blew a gasket and told her off. Oh no it wasn't that, I know it was Brian said it might be a gasket yes that's it. Super Sharon said mummy turning up late meant she could be mean and critical and so she meanly criticized the way Jennifer the cat sits. Sharon went like this she went 'They do say dogs take after their owners Kathleen, could you not go for deportment lessons somewhere to learn to sit in a ladylike manner? How else is Jennifer going to learn to sit nicely?' Mummy just smiled and wondered when she would have time to fit the deportment lessons in. Our Freya was her normal angelic self in her class and was happy when it was changeover time.

My mate Jet is so proud and so is his owl fellah Brian because he aced the fire jumps for the very first time in history on his fourth birthday and I went like this to him I went 'listen mate, I'll buy you a pint later to celebrate and let you have our Jennifer the cats secret about having a lie down if you promise to teach me how to not be such a wus.' and Jet went like this he went 'Timothy mate, you just have to keep working at it lad and one day you'll get there. It's taken me four years of hard graft with a top trainer to get where I am today mate, and me owl fella helped too. Now what time are you picking me up?'

Anyway so anyway the cat was allowed in for hula hoop training again and she does seem to be getting the hang of it but she's not as good as me or anything.

When it was home-time mummy handed over the blue paddling pool to Lou and Jo for Poppy the menace and then because mummy had filled up the radiator after Freya's class she just drove home. Tragedy struck not long after passing Tesco as mummy's temperature gauge suddenly and without warning your honour shot up to 'STOP THE CAR QUICK' mode and so she did. She was just sitting there wondering how long it would take for the chariot to cool down and what she was going to say to the dealer on Tuesday and what could she have for lunch and the meaning of life and everything and then June pulled up in front of her and then Lou and Jo pulled up behind her and she thought like this she thought 'Oh God I'm being kidnapped only there is no one to pay the ransom or anything' They decided against kidnapping though on the grounds that she had already supplied a blue shell paddling pool and some rather pleasant herbs so they helped her to fix the chariot.

Then we got escorted home by the armed police and all the emergency services and we had outriders as well with all the sirens going and everything or it could have just been June, Lou and Jo but I'm not sure but we did get home safely and mummy said thank you very much.

I will keep you updated on my ongoing adventures just as soon as I can.

Love Timothy. xxxx

* * * * * * * * * * * *

ABOUT THE AUTHOR

Timothy Conehead has an honorary degree from Liverpool John Moore's University and was shortlisted for the Nobel Peace Prize for Illiteracy in 2016. He is friends with the Liver Birds, coaches Sir Ken Dodd's Diddy men in the art of nonsense on Friday mornings and has agreed to be interviewed by his mate John Bishop in his new series to be screened later next year. He adores Craig Charles and is set to partner Danny John-Jules in the next series of Red Dwarf. He is a frequent visitor to Anfield and it is rumoured that he is currently in talks with Jurgen Klopp and could be the Reds secret weapon in the New Year. It has also just been confirmed that he will feature on Sir Paul McCartney's latest CD in 2017.

Only joking!!

Timothy is really clever and intelligent and needed a ghost writer to help him and so Sir Lord Jack of the Kingdom of Goodness and Love came back from Rainbow Bridge to help him when mummy was at work but he couldn't do it all and so we threw a bag of flour over mummy and put a white sheet over her so she could do some ghostly writing for me too! He has written to Santa Claus to ask for a new seesaw that will be kind to him and his dearest wish is to meet Paul O'Grady and to visit his farm to help him to round up his six sheep. Timothy dreams of being a factoid in the Steve Wright show preferably in the afternoon but time of day is not important. Laddie the Baddie came to help too and to make sue I put that nice picture of him in when he looks like he was being good and not a baddie.

In between doing ghostly writing for me and taking me to torture training mummy also is a hypnotherapist in the posh street in Liverpool just near the red light district where we think she plays games for money but we are not sure your honour they could be mind games or they could be any sort of games but I think she is on top of her game or on top in the game, I'm not sure now. She tells everyone she is a professional though and a nod is as good as a wink to a blind camel hiding in the cellar.

Mummy also writes about our unicorns and there is a series called 'Life on Belles Haven' and the unicorns are good and not naughty or anything and they are all for children but grown-ups like them too. Mummy writes lots of poetry I think it helps her to feel calm after trying to train us and saves her from needing therapy.

I can't find a really nice picture of mummy with our Laddie the Baddie so I am enclosing a picture of us all when we were the Fab Four and before our Jennifer had even been invented or was a twinkle in a working border collies eye or anything.

Mummy is also known as Kathleen Phythian but only when she answers the phone and then she goes like this, she goes " Kathleen Phythian how can I help you?" and then she talks to people about all her problems, no sorry she talks to people about their problems and then when she comes off the phone she is mummy again!

1. Sometimes she is called K.P. Nuts but please don't tell

anyone I told you that or I'll be hung drawn and quartered again and sent to clean the moat out followed by the slammer for me in this life, the next life and however many other lives I have to live your honour!

Thank you for reading my book, I hope it made you smile and remember,

All you need is Love

and a border collie or two or three or four or more.....

Love,
Timothy Conehead the Invincible!

It is all you need....

R.I.P.
Laddie the Baddie.

The prequel to 'Community Service' is called 'The Camel's Dead' and chronicles Timothy's journey from the moment he arrived at 'Love House' to be corrected.

or

If you are looking for amusing inspirational and motivational books for your little ones, suitable from as young as you can read to them up to top primary, why not have a look at the 'Life on Belles Haven' series. They are poetic stories about unicorns and all means of magical and quirky creatures all with good strong underlying values whilst still being fun. They are all written and illustrated by Kathleen and can be found in a number of libraries and on Amazon.

The Candyfloss Tree.

Unicorn Bridge.

A Tale of Two Unicorns.

Sparkle the Unicorn.

Twinkle the Unicorn.

Ruby the Christmas Unicorn.

Coming soon:-

Starburst the Unicorn.

Moonbeam the Unicorn.

www.ingramcontent.com/pod-product-compliance
Lightning Source LLC
Chambersburg PA
CBHW060614130626
46555CB00002B/516